When Her Hand Moves

When Her Hand Moves

For information, contact:
Villa Magna Publishing, LLC
4705 Columbus Street
Suite 300
Virginia Beach, VA 23462
www.villamagnapublishing.com

ISBN: 978-1-940178-52-3
Cover Design by Noel Hagman-Kiziltan
Editing by Noel Hagman-Kiziltan
            and Rocío Txabarriaga

Also by Omar Imady

Fiction
The Gospel of Damascus (novel)

Non-fiction
The Rise and Fall of Muslim Civil Society
The Syrian Uprising Domestic Origins and Early Trajectory (co-editor/co-author)
Syria at War, five Years On
Organisationally Secular: Damascene Islamist Movements and the Syrian Uprising (co-author)
When You're Shoved from the Right, Look to Your Left: Metaphors of Islamic Humanism

Coming in 2022
The Fear of Being Fearless (collection of short stories, read excerpt at the end of this book)
An Afternoon of Salt (book of poetry)
Simulated Encounters (novel)

Coming in 2023
The Unauthorised Biography of a Damascene Reformer

About the Author

Omar Imady was born in Damascus, Syria. He is an author, poet, and historian. His first novel, *The Gospel of Damascus*, was a *Book of the Year Award* finalist in 2012, and has been translated into French, Spanish, and Arabic. He has also authored and co-authored many books and articles on Syria and Sufism. He currently lives in the United Kingdom, between Scotland and Essex.

To Fatima, the Glowing One

"The hand is the visible part of the brain."

— *Immanuel Kant*

"your hand
touching mine.
this is how
galaxies
collide."

— *Sanober Khan*

"And the universe We designed by hand, and it is
We who are constantly expanding it."

— *The Winnowing Winds: 47*

Movement One

The Seduction of Jude

EVICTED

(1)

Saint Paul escaped Damascus in a basket lowered from a window, near a gate once dedicated to Saturn.

The year was 33 AD.

Jude Marsini escaped Damascus in a yellow Dodge Coronet, assembled at Hamtramck, Michigan.

The year was 2011 AD.

Over the last one thousand, nine hundred, and seventy-eight years, escape methods had significantly changed. But Damascus had not.

It was still evicting its best.

(2)

Abu Ammar was a Syrian Alawite. He was a carpenter. A plumber. A maker and seller of yoghurt. And the driver of the only surviving 1971 Dodge Coronet on the Damascus-Amman highway.

"Jude made a dangerous mistake today. He said things he should not have said. Please drive him safely to Amman. I have no one to ask this except you."

These were the words of Jude's father to Abu Ammar. They had known each other for years. Abu Ammar had relatives in all the branches of Syria's security agencies, and Jude's father had reached the conclusion, experientially, that in times of danger in Syria few things were more valuable than a well-connected driver.

Several years earlier, Abu Ammar had arrived unexpectedly at the Marsinis' home.

"My son is sick. He needs an operation. The hospital asked for 200,000 pounds. I have no one to ask this except you."

Jude's father signed a blank cheque.

"Take this and write the number you need."

(3)

It was ten thirty at night when Abu Ammar arrived at Jude's home in west Damascus. The day was Thursday, the 29th of September 2011. Nothing about this was arbitrary. By eleven forty-five, the Dodge would have crossed 105 kilometres and arrived at the Syrian-Jordanian border, exactly fifteen minutes before the day shift of the border officers was about to end. Not only were they tired of checking passports, they were also eager to leave and return home for the weekend. Those who had to work on Fridays and Saturdays, Syria's official weekend, did so on a biweekly basis. At midnight, they would finally return to their homes.

Jude Marsini's name was on the no-travel list. He was barred from leaving the country. Abu Ammar had studied the situation carefully and repeatedly, and in his mind, there were three factors that would–separately or collectively–guarantee Jude's safe passage out of Syria:

One, restless border officers who were eager to stamp their last passport and leave the border station.

Two, meeting one of his many relatives who worked as security guards at the border.

And three, the intervention of the Prince of the Bees.

The Prince of the Bees was Ali. The cousin of the Prophet of Islam. The Christ of the Alawite faith. His name was written in deep green on the boot of the Dodge Coronet.

When they reached the border, Abu Ammar asked Jude to stay in the car. One hour. Two hours. Three hours passed. Jude's mind bounced from fear to paranoia. He visualised the entire scene. His arrest. Torture. Life sentence. The fear knocked him like a hammer into sleep.

*

He awoke to sunrise. And a smiling Abu Ammar.

The computer server had gone down, and they needed to wait for it to be fixed. Of course, this was Syria, so nothing got fixed quickly. They said. Abu Ammar's friends had finally felt sorry for him and stamped their passports without a computer check. All the other passengers were still waiting.

"Who can resist the intervention of the Prince of the Bees?"

He said.

*

O Prince of the Bees
O Ali, the one who truly gives
Eternal and forgiver
The opener of the gate
I ask you by the five who were selected
And by the six who were manifested
The seven glowing stars
The eight powerful ones who carry the throne
The nine praiseworthy ones
The ten pure chickens
The eleven dawns of the gate
The twelve lines of authority...
I ask you to rid us of these physical temples
And adorn us, in their place, with garments of
light
That we may always glow
Amidst the celestial bodies.

An Alawite Prayer - The Compilation, Sura III

Jude Marsini, like his mother Sukayna, had a peculiar mental trait. He saw things at times in a manner that reflected intense, and involuntary imagination. Jude realised this about himself whilst still a child.

"Mama, I saw my teacher today wearing a clown's costume. I know this can't be true because by the end of class he was wearing his suit again. I think there is something wrong with me."

"Jude, there is something *right* about you. You have your mother's secret."

From the moment Abu Ammar crossed the border into Jordan, Jude would look out of the window and see only fields of lavender under the morning twilight. A violet continuum which replaced the otherwise barren desert landscape from the border to Amman. Cars racing by became formations of mountain bluebirds gliding along the highway. *Sialia currucoides*. He was experiencing his first moments of inner peace since he had realised that he had violated one of the ten commandments of the Syrian regime:

Thou shall not imply that anything could have been handled in a manner superior to how it was actually handled.

In Sukayna's library there were many books. A few she had purchased, but most she had inherited from Murad, her late uncle, a renowned Syrian scholar of Biology. Murad had been secretly possessed with ideas popular in nineteenth century Britain and America. Phrenology. Mesmerism. Spiritualism. His book collection reflected his uncommon intellectual pursuits. Murad was also a dedicated and proud member of a Masonic Lodge, named Ibrahim El Khalil Lodge No. 4, consecrated in Damascus in 1927. He was fortunate to die in 1963 right before Freemasonry was banned and Syria's long political nightmare began. Along with his books, Murad left his elaborate Masonic regalia to Sukayna, his beloved niece and only heir.

Jude would spend hours going through his mother's books, even as his brother and father entirely ignored them. Sukayna noticed this, so she read to him. At night. From books that were difficult even for native English speakers, since most were by authors who lived in the late nineteenth and early twentieth century. As her uncle had done with her, Sukayna would not bother to stop and help her son understand the many difficult words these books contained. He would follow her forefinger along the lines of the page, watching as she summoned the words to life. She would read as though Jude understood perfectly. In time, he did. The largest collection by one author belonged to Sir Richard Burton. But Jude's favourite books were those of William Samuel Furneaux. The pages of *The Out-Door World* flooded his mind with details of tropical adventures, exotic illustrations, and the most wonderful and obscure creatures. He learnt all their Latin names by heart.

As he looked out of the window at the fields of lavender his eyes were creating, the words of Hermes came back to him:

'As above, so below.'

*

(5)

Jude studied History at Princeton and completed a PhD in what his father regarded as a useless subject. Medieval Arabic palaeography. History professors at the University of Damascus were paid very little, and so Jude remained dependent on his father financially. As his older brother worked at the family's marble factory, Jude edited old manuscripts. At times, Jude's father would seem proud of him:

"You do what you are good at. I will always take care of you."

The default state, however, was frustration:

"These are your mother's genes. I know them well. You dedicated your life to things no one cares about. You could have studied architecture and made something beautiful from all this marble. Instead, you studied paper. Ancient paper!"

Yet, nothing was worse in the eyes of Jude's father than the words his son shared with his students. All three hundred of them. As they gathered in the large university auditorium for his Wednesday evening class. When asked what he thought of the protests, and how the government was responding, Jude first hesitated, aware that there were always several members of Syrian Security amongst his students.

"I think the situation could have possibly been handled with less violence."

Sukayna felt her son had answered wisely. After all, by September 2011, Damascus was buzzing with stories of killings, arrests, and torture. Jude's father, the man entrenched with survivalist Damascene genes, felt his son was reckless, and had placed himself and his entire family in danger.

"They will come after you. Then start harassing us."

*

Before Jude walked out of the house to meet Abu Ammar on the night of his escape, his father placed a large envelope in his pocket. Jude understood that this was meant to cover his expenses until something could be arranged. His father was unaware of the fact that Jude had quietly decided that this time he would not rely on his help. Instead of staying at a hotel, opening an account at a Jordanian bank and waiting for his father to send even more money, as he had promised, Jude decided to phone Rami.

"I will be arriving tomorrow in Amman. Would it be possible to stay with you for a few days?"

"My new clinic has an extra room with its own bathroom. You are welcome to stay in it for as long as you wish. Why stay a few days? Stay a few years."

(6)

Rami was a Jordanian dentist. Eman, his wife, a lawyer, was mechanically rational in her waking hours, and hopelessly lucid in sleep. Once, several summers ago, Eman started having a recurrent dream. She would see herself in Damascus searching for an old shop famous for its *boza*. Mastic ice cream. She would continue to wander through old Damascene alleys, lost, until a man appeared. He would guide her to the ice cream shop.

Rami felt her dream was easy to both fulfil and disprove. He would take her to Damascus. They would visit Bikdash, the famous Damascene boza shop. And they would *not* get lost.

He studied street maps of Damascus and asked several friends. He felt he knew the way perfectly. Yet, they *did* get lost. Instead of walking through the Hamidiyyah Souk, where Bikdash was located, they ended up wandering around Bzuriyyah with its rows of spice and candy shops. They stood in a cloud of aromas. Cinnamon. Camomile. Thyme.

Jude appeared, wearing a black suit. He owned twelve. Six tailored to austere perfection by Asia. Six tailored to modern elegance by Marina. To most Damascenes, Asia and Marina were competitors. To Jude, these Damascene suit makers were there to mirror his sensibilities.

As in her dream, Eman approached Jude.

"Excuse me, do you happen to know where Bikdash is located?"

Jude smiled.

"Come with me. It would be my pleasure to walk you to the best boza shop in Damascus."

"Not just Damascus. The whole world."

"Yes, you must forgive me. You see, to Damascenes, Damascus is the whole world."

He said.

If she was later asked, Eman would have said that was the moment when she realised that she was willing to follow this man anywhere.

*

Before going back to Amman, Rami and Eman lived for years in San Francisco. Rami even opened a private clinic there. Yet, on the very same day they discovered Eman couldn't have children, Rami decided they would go back to Amman. There was no rational link between Eman's infertility, and the need to return home. They didn't even have much of a family to go back to. It had been Rami's decision. It was a form of grieving. A desire to immerse oneself in the overwhelming process of moving and starting again. And so, they did.

At seven in the morning, Jude arrived at Rami's clinic, not too far from the Four Seasons hotel in west Amman. The clinic was on the first floor of a stone villa. White. Like all the other stone villas around it. As he said goodbye to Abu Ammar, he placed the large envelope in his pocket.

"Give this back to my father."

(7)

There are many words in Arabic that can be traced back to Aramaic. *Natur*, or caretaker, is one of them. Jude found the villa's natur standing outside the gate. He was an Egyptian man, eager to unlock the door of the clinic and return to a plump young woman wearing a colourful headscarf, standing at the bottom of the staircase.

Rami's clinic wasn't open on Fridays, and so Jude had the whole place to himself. As he walked inside, scenes inspired by John Collier, an eighteenth-century artist who had found his way into his mother's library, came to life before his eyes. A man screaming as a dentist extracts his rotten tooth with a string. When the string fails to work, the dentist reaches for a pair of pliers. More screaming. Jude walked faster.

Inside his room, the scenes and noise stopped. There was a bed. A bedside lamp. A small wardrobe. An all-white and minimalist room. Jude threw himself on the bed. In a matter of minutes, he was asleep. He dreamt of a swarm of bees chasing security guards at the border.

*

At noon, Jude was awoken by Rami's sonorous greeting:

"Welcome to Amman, the most boring city in the Middle East! Come, you must be hungry."

In ten minutes, they were at Abu Jbara, a chain of falafel restaurants scattered across the capital.

Rami ordered a feast. Falafel. *Hummus Beiruti*, a version of hummus with parsley popular in Beirut. Egyptian *ful*, or puréed fava beans. *Fattet Hummus*, a mixture of bread, chickpeas and yoghurt, with ghee and pine nuts added on the top. *Hummus Qudsiyyah*, a special from Jerusalem blending fava beans and chickpeas. Plates of pickles, bread and mint tea. The food felt warm, and the hard texture of the falafel complemented the smooth hummus. Jude would dip a falafel in the hummus and then immediately reach for a pickled hot pepper. The three different sensations—hard, soft, spicy—felt almost ticklish. He was easily seduced by contrasts. And very vulnerable to contradictions. Time passed. The waiters returned repeatedly with baskets of warm bread and pots of tea. As they inhaled the food, Jude shared his story in cathartic detail.

"And now that you are here, do you have a plan, Jude?"

"Have you heard of the American College of Amman?"

"The ACA? Yes, it's a new place attracting the spoilt

rich kids of west Amman."

"That's my plan."

*

Jude spent the rest of Friday walking. He walked from the clinic all the way to Rainbow Street near the First Circle. Rami had mentioned a place called Wild Jordan. It wasn't difficult to find. It had a café that overlooked the citadel and Jude sat there for hours reading the *Leaves of Grass* from a small leather-bound book. A gift from his mother.

Walking back, he thought about Damascus. His parents. His brother. His friends. He thought about the protestors who were being shot. Even during funerals. Faces came back to him. Like Ghiath Matar, the young man from the town of Darayya who gave out flowers and water bottles to security officers. A few days after he was arrested, his tortured dead body had been sent back to his pregnant wife. Jude remembered a professor of his at Princeton who loved to talk about theodicy and why bad things happened to good people. In Jude's mind, bad things were happening to very good Syrians. And while he felt blessed to be out of Syria, he understood well that all the heroes refused to leave.

Jude woke up early on Saturday morning. He hadn't brought with him everything he wanted from Damascus but did have those items he simply couldn't imagine himself without. A classic shaving set was one. Jude took this ritual very seriously. To most, Cecil B. Hartley was nobody. But to Jude, he was the unquestionable authority on all matters related to gentlemanly etiquette.

When it comes to shaving, the appropriate approach is to shave oneself. After all, Napoleon, as Hartley reminds us, would say:

"A born king has another to shave him. A made king can use his own razor."

Jude Marsini owned a Thiers Issard straight razor with a handle made of real snakewood. A graduation gift from his father. The brush was a pure grey Kent badger, which had its own maroon box. For shaving cream, he used a special homemade recipe consisting of olive oil, honey, Castile soap, and lemon and mint essential oils. He had a large glass bottle full of this exotic lotion. For aftershave, he was religiously loyal to Old Spice. The entire process took twenty minutes.

Since all his suits were black, the choice was only

between an Asia suit and a Marina. He chose an Asia for a more respect-demanding effect, and a gold Christian Dior tie. All his shirts were white, with long pointed double down collars. His black Tods double monk strap shoes, another gift from his father, completed the look. Jude was six feet tall. He had a fair complexion and dark chestnut hair.

Walking out of the villa, the words of Hartley came back to him:

'Carry into the circles of society a refined, polished manner... and it will meet you with smiling grace.'

(9)

The ACA, or the American College of Amman, was a branch of a Los Angeles-based university. It was only a year old and was located near the Fifth Circle. A five-minute walk from Rami's clinic. By nine, Jude had arrived at the ACA, and was waiting for someone to find the time to speak to him. He had explained to the receptionist that he was there to apply to teach at the college. She was barely older than twenty. She had a pencil stuck in her hair. She acted as though Jude's visit was a common event. Like he was one of hundreds she had previously encountered. She mumbled something about a 'Kumar' who may have the time to see him. A grey-haired man who fit the image of the Kumar Jude had imagined appeared suddenly. He had the look of a man who was perpetually tense. Like he had somehow been burdened with tasks and responsibilities that were neither doable nor adequately appreciated.

"You asked to see me?"

"Yes, my name is Jude Marsini. I am very interested in teaching here. This is my CV."

Kumar glanced at the paper. He shook his head. He was not impressed.

"We don't teach History here. My apologies. There

are no vacancies for you."

Kumar abruptly turned away from Jude. Someone had entered the room. Someone important enough for Kumar to replace his tense look with a smile, and to stand upright. Everyone in the room was suddenly standing. Jude turned around and saw a short man in a silver suit. He was surrounded by three men who looked and acted like bodyguards. The man walked towards Jude, as he distributed smiles to the students and staff who were staring at him. With his eyes fixed on Jude, he addressed Kumar.

"Who is this gentleman?"

"Your Excellency, this is..."

"My name is Jude. Jude Marsini."

"Yes, this is Dr. Marsini. He was asking if we had any vacancies."

Jude felt that the appropriate thing to do at this point was to hand his CV to the man who was acting and being treated like he was far more important than any academic title could possibly capture. He looked at the CV. This time there was a smile that clearly expressed approval.

"Princeton?"

"Yes, Your Excellency. My PhD is from Princeton."

Jude chose to refer to him as Kumar had.

The man in the silver suit turned to the three men surrounding him and repeated:

"Princeton."

The three smiled with approval too, though Jude doubted they understood what their boss was saying.

"Kumar, arrange for this gentleman to meet me in my office."

Jude had expected him to comment on his history major. Something along the lines of what his father would have said. Using words like irrelevant. Useless. Impractical. Kumar was now also smiling, as though the singular significance of Princeton had suddenly dawned on him.

"Yes, of course, Your Excellency."

The man and his bodyguards left the room. In minutes, the scene returned to its pre-excellency state. Kumar stared into space. Seconds passed. He pointed at a corridor.

"Please follow the signs."

He said.

A lift carried Jude to the twelfth floor where he found himself in yet another waiting room. This was far more prestigious. Several more men in dark suits were sitting on leather couches. In Jude's eyes, they stayed human for only a few seconds. By the time he had sat down, they were all penguins. Serious and sophisticated penguins who glanced infrequently at Jude with contempt. He was obviously not one of their own.

A golden plaque hung over a large, closed door:

H.E. Rashid Arsalan

Near the door, a woman sat behind a small desk. She was in her forties. Her left hand had rings on each finger. They glittered as she conducted the penguins to different doors. She was the undisputed queen of the chamber, who was treated and spoken to with utmost respect. Three hours passed. Countless penguins had arrived and departed. Then Rashid appeared, with the three men who seemed to constitute his human shadow.

"Ah, you are here. I will see you this evening."

He turned to the woman behind the desk, who was now standing.

"Souzan, I will have dinner with this gentleman at nine. You like Italian?"

Jude nodded quickly, though it was obvious that this was not the type of question that awaited a response.

The Romero restaurant was founded in 1979 by Flavia Romero, the daughter of an Italian surgeon assigned by a philanthropic foundation to help establish the first hospital in Amman. At eight thirty, Jude once again walked out of the clinic and headed towards the Four Seasons hotel in the hope of finding a taxi. Romero was in Jabal Amman, twenty minutes from Rami's clinic. Souzan had asked him to be there by nine. He arrived five minutes early. When he introduced himself, a waiter took his arm and directed him to a large table in one of the corners of the restaurant. To his left, a large antique mirror decorated the wall. Almost the moment he sat down, waiters rushed to the table with platters of antipasti. Placing the dish on the table, they would pronounce its name in hushed Italian tones.

"Parmigiana di melanzane. Funghi misti saltati e olio al tartufo. Capriccio di filetto…"

Jude felt overwhelmed. There were over eight dishes on the table. And all this was still in its first phase. Still, Rashid didn't come. Fifteen minutes passed. More waiters and more dishes.

"Penne all'arrabbiata. Ravioli al salmone. Tonnarelli all orientale…"

It was unthinkable for Jude to start eating before Rashid arrived. Sukayna and her books had produced a gentleman who had an acute sense of what should and should not be done. He began to feel embarrassed. Like he was on a date, but he was being stood up. Half an hour passed. The main dishes started to arrive. The waiters seemed oblivious to the fact that Jude was not eating. Nor did they seem to care that he was still alone at the table.

"Piccata di vitello al limone. Misto di pesce..."

The waiter was about to pronounce the name of the third main when it became clear that no innovative technique could make more space on the table for this dish. At that very moment, Rashid arrived. He was dressed in a light blue suit. He carried a majestic air and glowed with it. Jude, perplexed by the three men still standing behind him, stayed standing even as Rashid sat across from him. Rashid turned around and gestured for the men to leave.

*

"You haven't started eating. You can't ever wait for me. I'm always late. Let this be your first lesson tonight."

Though Rashid spoke with a British accent, Jude concluded that he must be Lebanese. *Arsalan* was a well-known Lebanese family, and the sophistication

Rashid carried seemed consistent with an upper-class Lebanese sensibility.

"Tonight, you eat. I will speak. By the time you finish eating, I will have shared with you everything. Agreed?"

"Yes, Your Excellency."

The ACA was a complicated setup. Rashid explained. The idea had been his. He had done everything: approached the head office in LA with the proposal. Purchased the land. Built the classrooms and the offices. Convinced all the Jordanian officials who had to be convinced. And there were many. Rashid had done all of this. In the beginning, they had appreciated what he did. But now things had changed. Now, they sent him people from LA. They wanted to run things.

"Even the Jordanian aboriginals—I call them aboriginals, you see, because sometimes they act like they just walked out of their tents—well, they too want to run things."

"Racist!" Jude's mother screamed in his head. But he ignored her and continued to attend keenly to Rashid's diatribe.

Rashid was convinced now that they were using the pretext of 'academic' to take the ACA away from him.

Even the American Ambassador was in on it. The message to Rashid was clear: as long as he got his share of the profits, he should just let them run it.

"The problem is, Dr. Marsini, if I let them run it, they will kill it in a month. Mark my words. One month."

Rashid stopped to inspect whether Jude was eating. He gestured to a waiter who rushed to the table.

"Bring us some espresso."

*

The espresso arrived. The waiter was forced to start clearing the table. Jude made it known that he was done, though he had only politely tasted some of the starters. Rashid lit a cigar and started talking again.

Rashid Arsalan had come from a family where failure was not an option. He didn't take anything for granted. This was why he could not let go.

With his first sip of espresso, Jude watched as Rashid morphed into Marlon Brando. Complete with cotton balls wedged against his lower gums. A red rose in his lapel. A large black signet ring worn, unexpectedly, on his middle finger. An occasional, chilling, smoke filled silence echoed in the hollows and recesses of Jude's mind.

*

Growing up in Damascus, Jude had always felt overwhelmed by the city's masculine imagery. From the photographs of the president, which came in various sizes from postage stamp to full size building reliefs, mandatory assertions of submission, to the orators of mosques screaming their sermons as though the louder their voices, the more authentic their claim to the sacred. And finally, to the way men took possession of the streets, from the way they walked, to the way they littered the doorways. Leaning. Staring. Claiming. As Jude caught sight of Rashid's ring, he recalled his abhorrence of it all.

*

Rashid took out another cigar from his pocket and handed it to Jude. Jude didn't smoke, but he was not going to refuse anything this evening. Somewhere between his unconsciousness and consciousness a thought was brewing: everything prior to this night he owed to his father. His education. His lifestyle. Even his escape from Damascus. This was his first chance to do something on his own.

"Dr. Marsini, I need a Rashid in disguise. They don't want Rashid, the Lebanese entrepreneur? Fine. I will give them Rashid, the Princeton graduate."

Rashid smiled, took a few sips of espresso, and blew smoke in the air.

"I have a few strong gifts. Perception is one of them. I can tell you what makes a man tick in a matter of seconds. You, for example, have clearly come from a comfortable background. You are not hungry. Not even for Italian food."

More smiles. Coffee. Smoke.

Jude Marsini was not hungry in the way that made Rashid feel he was capable of deceiving him. And yet he was ambitious. To Rashid, Jude fit the image of an aristocrat going through a difficult time. His aristocratic air made Rashid able to trust him in a way he couldn't trust the ravenous men that surrounded him. At the same time, the fact that he seemed to be going through a difficult patch made him reliable. Willing to do just about anything.

"I am as you describe, Your Excellency."

This time laughter. Followed by espresso and more smoke.

"Good. So, this is our deal. You are the new academic dean of the ACA. You are me in a different body. There are a few things that are important to me, and I will let you know what they are. You'll find a way to make them happen. Are you married?"

"No, Your Excellency."

"Divorced? Widowed?"

"No. I just cherish my own space too much to commit to a marriage."

"But you do like women?"

Jude ignored the scent of homophobia.

He did like women. He said. Though he tended to be too shy to start anything serious. His shyness had so far protected him from an otherwise inevitable marriage. His mother said. But he was forty now. And quite happy to be single.

Jude instantly regretted bringing up his mother. But Rashid was clearly digging deeper. And he seemed, so far, to like what he was unearthing.

"Perfect. I cannot tolerate the use of family as an excuse for incompetence."

Adel would be his driver. He would also be their go-between. Most of the time Jude would be doing what diplomats do: a constant balancing act. Making sure that everyone felt they were respected and appreciated. But every now and then, Adel would communicate instructions from Rashid. When he did, Rashid expected Jude to make them happen. He shouldn't act like he was Rashid's man, though everyone would presume he was. But he must never acknowledge this. In fact, he must often speak and act in ways that seemed to contradict it. Unless he received a message from Rashid asking him to do otherwise.

"And don't worry about sharing information with me. I know everything. There are cameras in every room at the ACA. And I love watching."

This time there were no smiles.

"Any questions?"

"No, Your Excellency. It's all very clear."

"Good. I very much dislike questions."

The ACA followed the Jordanian system: Sunday to Thursday. Jude was scheduled to start the next day. Rashid would be returning to Beirut for now. He would be back for Eid. He said. Sometime in early November.

Rashid stood up, signalling that the event had now ended. Jude was quick to stand too. They shook hands, and in a few seconds, the Godfather had made his exit.

(11)

Jude Marsini could not sleep. He left his bed and opened the window. It was cool and serene. His room looked out over the back garden. Opposite, and beyond the garden, there was an office building. It had reflective glass from the ground all the way up to its highest floor. The lack of lights from inside the building accentuated its grand mirror effect. Jude looked down and noticed how the glass perfectly reflected the scene from the villa's ground floor. He realised that he could see right inside the natur's home. The light was dim. But everything was clearly visible.

The natur was sitting on a couch across from his plump young wife. She had her feet on his lap. She was completely naked and seemed far more beautiful than she had when Jude had accidently seen her the day he first arrived. Her skin was the colour of wheat, her hair long, wavy and dark. They seemed relaxed. Certain that no one could see them. Perhaps trusting that the office building was always empty at night. The natur's hand was caressing her feet. One of her fingers was drawing circles on her leg. She seemed to be telling him a story. A few minutes passed. He pulled her towards him. Her body was now lying entirely over him. Her head resting between his neck and shoulder.

She was now reflected on the glass building like a Boucher painting. A portrait of an Egyptian Marie-Louise O'Murphy. Suddenly, the natur raised his hand in the air and then landed it forcefully on her bottom. This wasn't a tender act of affection. It seemed deliberate. Uninhibited. Her body jerked back. Her toes flexed, and pointed down towards the couch, giving away a tense conviction that this was not going to be a singular act. Jude's eyes were inventing details. But the basic scene was not his making. The violent hand continued its work, and with each time it landed on her, Jude whispered a number, as though counting on her behalf.

She raised her head. Her mouth was open, and her eyes stared directly at the glass. Jude was convinced she was staring at him, pleading for him to come and save her from what was about to follow. "Eight" followed. Jude turned away from the window and got into his bed.

SELECTED

(1)

Rami usually arrived early at his clinic. But long before he got there, Jude was already on his way to the ACA. He found only a security guard standing near the door. A large man with a bushy black moustache, who introduced himself as Abu Shanab, or 'Father of the Moustache'. Abu Shanab led Jude to his new office. A room on the twelfth floor with large windows overlooking Amman. There was a partition separating it from Rashid's office, which seemed as though it had been installed overnight. Like his room at Rami's clinic, the furniture was white and scarce. It seemed clean enough to serve as a laboratory. There was a large folder on his desk with information on every possible thing the ACA did or wanted to do in the future. An espresso machine in the corner meant that Jude should not expect a secretary to show up asking him if he wanted coffee. Opposite his desk, and right below the ceiling, a small black camera was fixed to the wall. A faint red light indicated it was on. And recording. As Jude was staring at the camera, a tall man walked in.

"You'll get used to it. We all found it strange in the beginning, but it's comforting to know that no one is excluded. Even Abu Shanab has a camera pointed at where he stands in the parking lot."

Jude shook his head but didn't respond.

This was Walid. The man designated by Rashid to ensure that Jude knew how to navigate himself through this academic maze. Kumar, who was officially now Jude's deputy, was far too bureaucratic to be helpful for the types of tasks Rashid expected Jude to perform.

"Today, we will meet the staff. We can do that right now if you are ready. At eleven, we meet the professors. And before the day ends, we will have an assembly with all the students. We do this every week, usually on Sundays. Another unpleasant thing you need to get used to."

Jude smiled.

"My advice is to speak a lot. If you don't, they will. And everything they say will be meant to embarrass you. In most cases, you will find that my advice will be to speak very little, but not today."

By five, Jude had met them all. And though he did talk a lot, they listened eagerly. Even the students. Jude was eloquent. He could talk for hours about interesting topics. Learning styles. Personality types. The future of higher education. Back at his office, he found Adel waiting for him. Adel had silver hair and the stature of a lieutenant. It appeared as though fate had misplaced him as Rashid's driver. Though perhaps not. After all, he wasn't only a driver. He was also a messenger. And the messages he conveyed were battlefield strategies, straight from the office of General Arsalan.

*

Jude wanted to sit next to Adel in the S550 navy Mercedes, but Adel objected and asked him to sit in the back. Jude didn't argue. He understood that he was supposed to live up to a certain image, and this particular detail was apparently part of it. Adel drove towards Abdoun, away from the Fifth Circle and Rami's clinic. Minutes later, he stopped at a villa that was only a few blocks behind the American embassy.

"We have relocated you here. Let me introduce you to Ayşe. She's the caretaker of this place. Her husband was Dr. Arsalan's pilot, but he died a year ago. Not in an airplane crash. He died from a sudden stroke."

Adel walked in front of Jude and knocked on the door. A woman wearing a headscarf and carrying a young child opened it. A young girl appeared and stood next to her.

"Siti Ayşe, this is Dr. Marsini. Please take care of him. He is very important to Dr. Arsalan."

Ayşe smiled, and gestured for Jude to enter. Adel, who seemed very familiar with the place, walked ahead of them towards what he called 'the guest chamber'. It resembled a suite in a luxury hotel. A large bedroom. A bathroom with a jacuzzi tub. A window that overlooked the back garden. The furniture was elaborate and colourful. Very unlike his room at Rami's clinic.

"I will leave you now. Siti Ayşe is a great cook. I'm sure she has prepared you a wonderful dinner."

It was as Adel closed the door behind him that the ending of Jude's journey out of Damascus finally arrived to meet him.

(2)

Jude was suddenly alone. He opened one of the wardrobes and found it packed with black suits. To the far right, he noticed the ones he had brought with him. In addition, there were at least eight more. All made by Massimo Dutti. In the second wardrobe, he found white shirts. All with long pointed double down collars. There were also several new bottles of Old Spice placed neatly on one of the shelves. On the bed, Jude noticed there was a large brown envelope. It seemed to contain a book. As he started to open it, the young girl walked in and silently sat on the bed. She had a beautiful, delicate face. A tanned complexion. Long black hair. She wore a white linen nightdress. Outside, the weather could get cold after dark even in September. But the villa was well insulated, and the temperature was set to a warm twenty-two. Jude smiled as the young girl made herself comfortable. She acted as though it was perfectly normal for her to be there with him.

Inside the envelope there was a hard-bound leather book. *Mormonism: History, Theology and Sects.* There was also a smaller white envelope, and a stack of fifty-dinar notes. There seemed to be at least a hundred. Five thousand dinars. Around seven thousand dollars. Jude made these calculations quickly in his head. He felt his heart beat faster. The white envelope contained a note.

Ayşe is one of the few people you can fully trust. Use the money to settle in. - Rashid

The girl spoke.

"Dinner is ready. Come with me."

She said.

*

Jude wondered if she was supposed to have said this earlier, but deliberately postponed the announcement so she could get to observe him. Or perhaps she just enjoyed lying on his bed. The food was served in a room near the kitchen on a large oak table. There was only one plate, surrounded by several bowls. All glass. All small.

"I hate *mulukhiyya*."

The young girl, who was already sitting on a chair across from him, glared at the dish.

Mulukhiyya is the Arabic word for the leaves of *corchorus olitorius*. When cooked, the result is a dark green, and bitter dish that resembles a seaweed soup. It's not difficult to understand why a child would not like it. But Jude loved it. Especially when drenched with lemon juice.

"My name is Jude."

"I know. But Mother said I should only call you 'Doctor'. What kind of doctor are you? I hope you are not a dentist. I hate dentists."

Jude could hear Ayşe in the kitchen. But she had still not made an appearance.

"I guess you could say I'm a doctor of the past."

"Mother talks like that sometimes. She says strange things no one understands."

"And you? What is your name?"

"Guess!"

"I'm not really good at guessing... Şirin?"

"No fair. Adel must have told you."

"It's written on your pendant."

Her hands reached quickly to her gold necklace and placed it inside her night dress.

"You weren't supposed to see that."

Ayşe walked into the room, still carrying her baby who seemed to be always silent, as though in constant deep sleep. Jude wondered how she managed to cook and serve him dinner with a baby attached to her arm. She was wearing white prayer clothes that covered her body completely. Except for her face and hands. This was the first time he had looked directly at her. Her skin was much lighter than her daughter's. Her large eyes were emerald green. She was tall. And clearly very slim.

"Yes, her name is Şirin. She will be seven in a month."

"And I expect a present."

"Şirin, be polite."

"My baby sister has an ugly name."

"Şirin, stop! This is Batul. She will be one in December."

Jude had already noticed that all the dishes on the table were made of glass. But when he reached to his fork, he realised that the cutlery too was glass. He had never seen a glass fork before. And probably only a ceramic spoon. Şirin noticed him staring at his fork.

"Everything here is glass. Mother forbids anything else. She hates plastic the most though."

"Şirin, I don't hate anything. I just prefer glass."

Şirin looked at Jude fiendishly and repeated:

"She hates plastic."

Jude focused on his mulukhiyya.

*

Lying on his bed, he opened Rashid's book on Mormonism. Three pages in, the door opened. It was Şirin, carrying a cup of tea.

"Mother said this is very good for you. It's a very special tea. Make sure you drink it."

She said this and got on the bed next to him.

"I will leave when you finish your tea."

Jude took a sip. It was sweet. Milky. Warm. He looked to his right at the body lying next to him. The feet pressed against each other. The tanned complexion. The night dress pulled well above her knees. The hands playing with the pink strings that fell out of a small white bow near the collar.

"I'll leave you now. Mother said I still can't kiss you goodnight though."

*

Ayşe placed Batul in a white cot that was in the corner of a light green room. The girls' bedroom. Şirin's brass bed was right next to the window. Ayşe leaned over and kissed Şirin's forehead. Before leaving the room, she stood near the door. She placed her right hand on her mouth. With her eyes closed, she repeated a prayer. She moved her hand away. And blew.

(3)

Jude awoke to the voice of Şirin. It was still not six thirty. He knew this because that's when his alarm was set for and it had yet not gone off. She placed a cup of tea next to him and left smiling. This tasted much stronger than the one he had before he slept. It was flavoured with several strong spices. Cardamon. Anise. Orange blossom. It wasn't a latte. But it wasn't difficult to get used to.

In the dining room, a typical Syrian breakfast awaited him. Olives. Thyme with olive oil. Feta cheese. A boiled egg. He wondered if this was in his honour. Perhaps it was just very similar to a Turkish breakfast. Ayşe was wearing the same white prayer clothes, hemmed with tiny green flowers that she left strewn through the house as she walked. *Alchemilla mollis.* This morning her long white skirt was raised slightly above her ankles. The subtle had always been far more obvious to Jude than the obvious. Şirin was sat at the table in her school uniform. Navy pinafore. Sky blue blouse. Yellow ribbon.

"Doctor, promise you'll be here when I come back."

Outside, he found Adel standing next to the Mercedes, smoking a cigarette. Jude sat in the backseat trying to reconcile the lingering aftertaste of the tea with the aromas of his ride. Leather. Tobacco.

Heavy cologne.

"You have a meeting today at two with Salem Abdallat, the Jordanian Director of Accreditation. I will be waiting outside for you at one forty. This is from Dr. Arsalan."

A small white envelope. A note:

Focus, and listen attentively. Abdallat is as sly as a fox.

*

Jude spent most of the day with Walid and Kumar going through the accreditation files. Hours passed. Pondering over the immense sea of paperwork made the reasons for meeting with Abdallat evidently clear.

Abdallat was obviously clever. But he was also suspicious. Or, at the very least, overly curious. He could explain exactly how the ACA needed to conform to the Ministry of Education's standards in order to protect its accreditation status. Carefully, he presented to Jude the anatomy of the accreditation system.

"For every hundred students, you must hire five professors. Every additional twenty students enrolled require, in turn, the hiring of another professor. So, a thousand students would mean you need..."

"Fifty professors."

"Exactly. You learn quickly. So, now explain this to me, Dr. Marsini: given this ratio, why would the ACA present us with student numbers that would require it to add far more professors than the actual number of students we have on our records would necessitate?"

"There must be a misunderstanding. Let me get back to you on this."

"Okay, Dr. Marsini. You're new, I understand. You see, most universities do everything they can to avoid hiring new professors. Even if they must creatively make it seem that their student body is smaller. Your university appears to be doing the exact opposite."

"I'm sure this is a misunderstanding."

"Well, let's hope by next Monday you'll be equipped enough to clear up this misunderstanding."

*

"Read to me."

Şirin lay on Jude's bed. She was wearing a long, light blue night dress. Her hair was wet. It smelled like eucalyptus.

"I am he that walks with the tender and growing night,
I call to the earth and sea half-held by the night."

(4)

Jude woke up several times during the night. He felt warm and opened the window to invite in the fresh air. He knew he had been having strange dreams. But they eluded him now.

The thought of breakfast seemed unpleasant. He drank his tea. He found Ayşe sitting on the couch nursing her child. She quickly covered her breast with her long prayer scarf, scattering more green flowers.

"I'm sorry, I should have said something."

"No, it's okay, I just wasn't expecting you this early."

*

In the car, Adel handed him another envelope. Bigger. Heavier.

"We have an unexpected meeting this evening. We thought it would be next week, but we got confirmation last night. Prince Ali will meet you at six. We can either come back here first or leave straight from work."

"I think I would rather come back for a few minutes to freshen up."

Jude opened the envelope and found the *Seven Pillars of Wisdom* by T.E. Lawrence. And a note:

Take a long lunch break and read as much as you can before your meeting with the Prince.

All day, Jude remained captured by the scene of Ayşe nursing. The contrast between the slimness of her frame and the fullness of her breast. Between her tracing paper complexion and the dusty rose of her nipple. The way her breast collapsed when she suddenly moved Batul away from it, right before she covered herself with her prayer scarf. That particular frame captured him the most. He tried his best to engage with Walid. To read about the desert adventures of Lawrence during lunch. But the scene kept retuning. It wasn't sensual as much it was maternal. That was the strangest thing of all. It made him want to ask his mother an embarrassing question:

Mama, was I nursed?

This was his first message to Damascus since his arrival.

*

Adel drove him home. Jude was eager to see Ayşe again. He found Şirin studying at the table.

"You came back."

"Yes, but only for a short while."

"Mother is out but she asked me to make you a cup of tea."

"It's okay, I'll have some when I come back."

"Sorry. She insisted. You don't want me to get into trouble, do you?"

Jude put on a new suit and chose a pine green tie.

"Here you go, Doctor. Your tea."

"You make it just as good as your mother."

"The truth is I just heated it up. Mother wouldn't trust me with your tea."

It was warm. Easy to drink fast. Jude sat his cup down. Şirin hugged his legs. He reached down and lifted her up. She became a goldfinch. *Carduelis*. Perched on his arm. She pecked his shoulder.

"Are you wondering why I can hug you now?

"Should I?"

(5)

Prince Ali was in his sixties. He spoke like a professor from Oxford. There seemed to be no topic that he couldn't discuss with authority. He was clearly a proud Hashemite. So distant were the unpolished Baathists with their endless discussions of conspiracies from a man of this type. Prince Ali invited Jude to attend his weekly literary salon, which took place at seven every Tuesday. Jude promised he would. He hoped Rashid would be happy with this. It implied that he had made a good impression on the Prince.

(6)

Ayşe was not wearing her prayer clothes. Like her daughter, she was wearing a night dress. They were sat on the couch. Her hair was tied up in a bun. It was chestnut. With red undertones. Jude stopped at the door. Seconds passed. He wondered if he was supposed to apologise. They were both smiling at him. He walked into his room without a word.

"Aren't you going to sit with us, Doctor?"

"Should I?"

"We were waiting for you!"

He left his tie and jacket on his bed but decided against pyjamas. He returned to the lounge looking awkward and confused.

"Your tea is ready."

Even Ayşe's voice seemed now to have lost its formal tone. She was warm. Relaxed. Like she hadn't been since he arrived.

Jude had trouble looking at the pair directly. His head tilted downwards, staring at the floor.

"Dr. Arsalan wants us to go to the Dead Sea on Friday.

He reserved rooms for us at the Movenpick. Have you been to the Dead Sea?"

"No."

"Good, Şirin and I are looking forward to this. It will stop you looking so tense."

Jude stood up and turned towards his room.

"Wait, aren't you going to kiss me goodnight?"

He bent down and went to kiss Şirin on her head. She moved her face quickly and kissed him on his cheek. It felt tender. Wet. Heavy with the scent of strawberry flavoured chewing gum. He would find the bubbles she blew floating around the sitting room early the next morning.

(7)

Jude woke up to Şirin trying to braid his short hair.

"I made sure your alarm was on silent."

Ayşe was laying breakfast on the table. She was still in her navy night dress. Last night had not been a dream. Though this fact only served to make the event more confusing. The dramatic change was not comfortable. The lack of explanation was unnerving. If he hadn't been afflicted with a chronic shyness from birth, Jude would have asked Ayşe directly. Perhaps he would at the Dead Sea, he thought to himself. He knew he wouldn't.

Adel reminded him of his virtual conference scheduled with Los Angeles. The ACA's headquarters in LA were finally going to meet their new dean in Amman.

He spent the day going through student files with Walid. Exactly how many students the ACA in Amman had. That was what he was after. A simple question, he thought. With a single, straightforward answer. There turned out, in fact, to be at least four. None of them was fully convincing.

There were active students. Inactive students. Students fully enrolled. Students with enrolment pending. Jordanian students. Non-Jordanian students. Students who had expressed interest in attending ACA. Those who had followed up on this interest. Copious classifications. The number of students ranged from anywhere between five hundred and one thousand.

"There has to be a way of knowing exactly how many students we have."

"Even if you and I went into each one of our classes and manually counted them, Jude, we would still not have accounted for those who are taking classes online. Or those who were simply absent."

"But we can't not know."

"Well, this is why we have so far used the highest possible number."

"Yes, but this means hiring professors we don't even need. It doesn't make sense."

"The difference between us, Jude, is that I've learnt to expect things not to make sense. You still think they should."

*

The Skype conference with LA was arduous. Roger, the Dean of Global Programs, spent most of the time talking about Princeton. His daughter had just been accepted there. His questions for Jude were relentless. An hour and forty-five minutes passed. Jude finally managed to ask for a full printout of all registered students at ACA Amman. This Roger promised to send soon.

Jude decided to work more on the students' files instead of returning home. He worked late, until after seven. The silent blinking of the camera was interrupted by a beep from his phone.

It was from his mother:

No, I couldn't nurse you. The milk never came. Missing you terribly. Your father and brother are unbearable without you.

8

"You are invited to dinner this evening at the American Ambassador's residence. We will go straight from work. We need to be there at five."

Adel handed him another envelope:

Focus on Zina. If she is on our side, no one else matters.

*

Outside, the Ambassador's residence seemed like a fortress. Several security checks had to be passed before reaching the main door. A young woman asked Jude to follow her.

Inside, a man dressed in a grey suit walked towards him.

"You must be Jude. I am Oliver Hyde."

"Pleased to meet you, sir."

"Oliver, please."

"Oliver."

Jude was led into a long room with a high ceiling.

Marble floors. No windows. There were several leather couches and chairs. A black piano. A glass table in the corner.

The woman in a black sleeveless dress who now walked into the room did so with such confidence that Jude noticed that even the walls bowed as she passed.

"And this is my wife, Zina."

Had she done anything other than proffer her hand for Jude to kiss, Cecil B. Hartley would have been surprised. Her fingers were remarkably warm against Jude's lips. Her ring remarkably cold. Seeing her smiling as he raised his head again, Jude was relieved. He had clearly done this right.

Oliver took a seat opposite Jude and Zina on one of the couches. A waiter arrived with glasses of orange juice.

"We always have orange juice before dinner. I hope you don't mind."

"Not at all."

A discussion on the ACA followed. Oliver was adamant at explaining his vision of what he wanted it to become. Something on par with the American University of Beirut. His mobile rang. Oliver excused himself. Jude focused on his orange juice. Moments passed.

"I must leave for an urgent meeting. Please do forgive me. I insist you stay and have dinner as planned. Zina is an excellent hostess."

"I had a feeling this would happen. Do you ever get such feelings, Jude?"

"Not this time."

Jude followed her.

*

In the year 1830, Joseph Smith founded the religion of Mormonism. He was only twenty-four. He was killed by an angry mob that stormed into the jailhouse where he was imprisoned. He was only thirty-eight. He left behind a legacy that some would call fascinating. One of sacred literature and scholarly intrigue. He also left behind forty-nine wives, possibly, and five surviving children, officially. Mormonism has been described as America's only true, unique, and intrinsic religion.

*

"Did they tell you we were Mormon?"

Rashid's book now made sense.

"Oliver belongs to the mainstream Church. But my faith would not be accepted by the Church at all. I don't think it would be accepted by anyone."

Jude wondered why she chose the kitchen for her theological confession. His awkwardness was ameliorated only by his knowledge of the fact that he was supposed to behave even more diplomatically than her husband.

"It's all about Joseph Smith in the end. How you understand him."

In the faith of Zina, Joseph was, to the Church, as Mormon men are now. Polite, God fearing gentlemen, upright in every possible way. Like her husband. The fundamentalists embellished this image only with polygamy.

"The problem is Joseph was so much more than all of this. In fact, he was none of this."

Jude's head spun. He was trying to recollect every word he had read about the Mormon prophet. He wanted to appear, at the very least, an educated listener.

"None of this?"

At length, Zina went on to describe to Jude how Joseph Smith had not been a gentleman at all. At least not in the way her husband was. Joseph was almost an anarchist. Willing to tear down worlds that had been established for centuries. And more than this: Joseph was as gnostic as they come.

"Gnostic?"

"Willing to reach out to Freemasonry, the Kabbalah, even the occult to help us understand the mystery of the divine. Now, it's time for a woman to do this. Are you hungry?"

Jude wondered if this was a trick question. He had been invited for dinner after all.

"I'm hungry if you are."

"I had a feeling you would say that. Would you like some coffee?"

Mormonism: History, Theology and Sects had made it very clear that adherents of the faith were prohibited from drinking coffee. From imbibing any form of caffeine, for that matter.

"Coffee?"

"Well, it's like coffee. Let's call it Mormon coffee."

Zina reached to a phone that was hanging from the wall. With a push of three buttons and the delivery of seven words, dinner plans were cancelled.

"You see that's one way I'm like Joseph. He clearly hated rules."

Whatever rules Joseph had shared, he clearly didn't stick to, at least according to the Ambassador's wife. Most Mormons would disagree with this.

"The funny thing is I think this makes him far more endearing. Have you heard about *The Book of Abraham*?"

"Yes. A little."

"This is a good example of what I mean. Taste your coffee."

Jude stared at the cup. He ran his fingers over the peculiar symbol on its side. An astronomical chart of some sort, and an inscription in what appeared to be Hebrew.

"Whatever you drink from this cup is permissible. The cup makes it so. Not the contents."

Jude took a sip. It had a strong taste of chicory. A hint of liquorice. There was also something else. Something he couldn't identify.

"That's very strong."

"You like it?"

"It's very different. Almost… medicinal."

"Perfect. That's the intended effect."

She returned to *The Book of Abraham*. Part of the Mormon Canon. Officially, the God-inspired translation by Joseph Smith of Egyptian papyri. Officially. Joseph had even completed a drawing that was partially preserved in the papyri.

"More coffee?"

Jude suspended his sense of taste and gulped the remaining black liquid in his cup.

"Sure."

"Are you planning on saying yes to everything I propose?"

Jude stared at Zina. Three black swallowtail butterflies flew out of her hair. *Papilio polyxenes*. They circled her head. Twice. Then her ankles. Two of them fluttered upwards and disappeared into her dress. One glided towards him. It hesitated, then floated down and rested at the bottom of his cup. Zina refilled his coffee. Jude swallowed the contents in one gulp.

At precisely three forty-five that afternoon, Zina had decided that no animals should be sacrificed at her behest that day.

"I'm not a vegetarian, but there are times, like today, when I just can't brush aside the image of a lamb seconds before it's slaughtered. There are times, mind you, when I wake up at night craving steak tartare."

They would eat omelette. She would prepare it. Judging from what he was drinking, Jude was not expecting a regular omelette. For a few brief seconds, he allowed himself to examine the woman at the stove. Athletic. Broad shouldered. A freckled complexion. Her hair was short, blond, and curly. Quite possibly bleached.

"Stop staring."

Her back was still turned.

"My Mormon underwear is invisible, in case you were wondering."

Had Jude managed to finish the book Rashid had given him, he would have read the section on Mormon attire which detailed the specific requirements for 'temple garments'. White undergarments which covered the shoulders and reached to the knees. Jude chose to hide both his embarrassment and confusion by examining, once again, the markings on his cup.

"Mormons were quite content with the Book of Abraham until the 1960s, when they discovered what Joseph had done."

Upon examination of the papyri that Joseph translated from Reformed Egyptian, and the document that detailed how he went about it, scholars concluded that the actual contents of the papyri had nothing to do with Joseph's translation.

"Nothing?"

"There's no such thing as Reformed Egyptian."

*

Two more swallowtails flew out of Zina's hair.

"To the unfaithful, this discovery meant that Joseph was a fraud. To the faithful, it's the scholars who got it wrong."

"What do you think?"

"That they're all missing the point. Who cares about what the papyri say? That's history. What matters is Joseph."

In Joseph's eyes, an ordinary papyrus had become sacred text. The very words of Abraham.

"The Book of Abraham is in fact an invitation to interact with the world in the same way."

"I'm not sure I understand."

Zina placed two plates on the table and sat very close to Jude. The scent of garlic and oil was overwhelming. Jude was trying very hard to stay in command of the moment. More swallowtails emerged.

"It's spicy. I hope you don't mind."

"It looks very colourful."

"I'll go back to Joseph after you have your first bite."

Each forkful was a natural continuation of whatever it was that had begun with the black liquid, three full cups of which Jude had so far drunk. Fighting the scents, spices, and scenes, he formed his face into a picture of appreciation.

"Ah, good, I'm relieved. I was worried it was all too much for you."

He felt her knee touch his leg. This could, of course, be easily explained as a natural occurrence at a table this small. If one were looking for an explanation.

"You know how with Midas, everything he touched became gold? Well, with Joseph, everything he touched became sacred. Anything and anyone could become part of something profound. Worthless papyri became the words of Abraham. A woman, even a married woman, became a person to whom he was sealed for eternity. Commerce, an insignificant town in Illinois became Nauvoo, the most sacred city in North America. This is what Joseph is. To me."

As she uttered these last words, Zina placed her hand over his. Jude felt her breath before her lips. Her scent arrived, despite the strong competition of garlic and oil. White musk. Jude closed his eyes, as though declaring his surrender. Whatever this was, he couldn't resist it. But nothing else followed. He opened his eyes again. She was sitting back. Smiling.

"You do realise we are supposed to do this every week."

"Every week?"

"Perhaps next time, I will be silent long enough for you to say something about the ACA."

Jude knew he was now being politely asked to leave. He stood up and followed Zina to the door. Her hand rested on the handle.

"I wasn't too hard on you, was I? It's just that whenever I see a beautiful man, I have to pray for grace."

*

He found Şirin reading on his bed. Lying on her stomach with her feet in the air.

"Are you going to come back this late every day?"

Jude glanced at his watch. It was only eight thirty.

"I'll try not to."

Jude washed his face several times. The problem

was that the scents he was trying to get rid of were inside of him. He splashed his face with some Old Spice, hung up his suit and put on his pyjamas. Şirin, who had left to inform her mother of Jude's arrival, returned with a cup of tea.

"You know we are leaving tomorrow morning to the Dead Sea?"

"Yes. Your mother mentioned this."

She lay down next to him. This had become their night-time ritual. She leaned her head against his arm, as he sipped Ayşe's milky tea. It felt soothing after Zina's spices. There are times when everything is far too surreal to be processed rationally. This was the case tonight. Jude finished his tea and closed his eyes. He fell asleep before Şirin left the room.

*

In his waking hours, Jude struggled with reality. In sleep, reality struggled with him. That night, he was back in Zina's kitchen watching swallowtails disappear beneath her dress. This time, there were hundreds. This time, he left his chair. Crossed the kitchen. He knelt behind her. His gaze followed the butterflies' path of flight. They disappeared between her legs. He inched his head up further beneath the pleats.

"My God, it's full of stars."

9

From the villa in Abdoun to the Movenpick at the Dead Sea, it was around fifty kilometres. Adel drove fast on the downhill winding road. Jude felt relieved to be sitting in the front. It wasn't hard for him to get motion sickness. Ayşe wore a long mustard dress and a white scarf. She sat in the back with her daughters. Şirin was wearing a red dress. Cotton. With polka dots. Batul was sat in a car seat between them. It was remarkable how quiet Batul was. Since he arrived, Jude didn't think he had heard her cry once.

The further down they drove, the more humid it became. Wet air. Like a steam bath in the desert. The Movenpick is located on the shores of the Dead Sea. It was the very definition of the colour of sand.

"You are all checked in. I'm going to a mosque nearby for Friday prayer, then heading back to Amman. I will be back tomorrow morning. Would you like to come to the mosque with me, Dr. Marsini?"

Jude was surprised by Adel's question. Though his father did go to Friday prayer, Jude didn't. Like his mother, he didn't practice the Islamic faith, though also like his mother he still identified himself as a Muslim. But this was more about belonging to a community than to a worldview. It had taken precisely eleven arguments for his father to stop talking to him about these things, and his mother simply never brought it up. Jude was convinced his mother was exactly like him: open to spiritual experiences, but entirely closed to religion.

"You have two neighbouring rooms. You can even open them up to each other, if you wish."

Adel said this as though it was a joke and he laughed. But no one else did.

The balcony of the rooms overlooked a beautiful rose garden. Further out was the sea. Further still was the horizon. In minutes, Şirin had found a way to open the door to their adjoining rooms.

"We need to keep this door open, Doctor. So we can make sure you are behaving."

"Şirin, be polite."

"I'm joking, Mother."

"You can shut the door if you wish, Jude. I don't mind if it's open."

"No, it's fine. I don't mind either."

Ayşe unbuttoned her dress. Three quick flicks of her long, slender fingers. Batul instantly reached to her breast. This was done, somewhat surprisingly, without the slightest air of discomfort on Ayşe's part.

"You two go and find some lunch. I'm going to feed Batul."

Jude ended up eating only salad and cheese from the buffet. Şirin ate a little of almost everything, and a lot of ice cream. When they returned to the room, Batul was still in her mother's lap, but Ayşe seemed as though she had fallen asleep. Jude was about to leave when Ayşe's eyes opened.

"Did you enjoy the lunch?"

"Yes, it was very good. But you haven't eaten."

"I will eat later. Let's head to the beach. You are going to get into the water, right?"

*

In the Dead Sea, there are specific rules one must abide by:

One, do not allow the water to enter your eyes.

Two, expect to feel a burning sensation if you have a small wound.

And three, forget about trying to swim as you would in any other sea.

Ayşe explained all this clearly to Jude before he entered the water.

"If you let the water carry you, you will enjoy it. If you try to swim, your body will roll, and you will end up with your head wet."

As is the case with all such rules, they are only helpful in retrospect. Jude violated all of them. In the process, he learnt to abide by all of them. Şirin was well versed in the art of Dead Sea swimming. She accurately described it as 'floating'. She laughed as Jude struggled to open his eyes, which burned with the strong saltwater. Ayşe stayed on land with Batul in her lap. She was dressed in a black body suit and a sheer white sarong. Over her scarf, she wore a large white hat. When Jude appeared to have become less prone to rolling in the water, Şirin took hold of his hand.

"Come. Let's swim towards the sun."

He followed her. They used each other for balance. The breeze was light and cool. With every step the water became less of an enemy. The sun was strong, but somehow it made Jude feel safe. For a minute, for a brief minute, as he held Şirin's hand and looked west at the distant horizon, it all felt too beautiful to be taking place on earth.

When they were finally back in their room, and after

they had all changed, Şirin produced a box.

*

On the 16th of November, Muhammad ibn Ali ibn
Muhammad ibn Arabi al-Hatimi passed away. The
year was 1240. He was better known as Muhyiddin
ibn Arabi. Most say he was a Sufi master. Mystic.
Philosopher. Poet. Some say he knew God.

His teacher, Fatima of Cordoba, was said to be able
to command the words of revelation to carry out her
commands.

She could turn water into oil.

It was said.

She took great pleasure in playing the tambourine.

It was said.

"There is no creature in the universe more powerful
than the woman—for each angel that God has created
from the breath of women is the most powerful of
angels."

Ibn Arabi said.

*

"So, what are we playing?"

"Snakes and Ladders. Don't worry I'll teach you."

"I know how to play, Şirin."

Şirin smiled.

"Not this Snakes and Ladders. This is Mother's version."

"Well, it's not made up by me. I just sewed the words and designs onto the fabric."

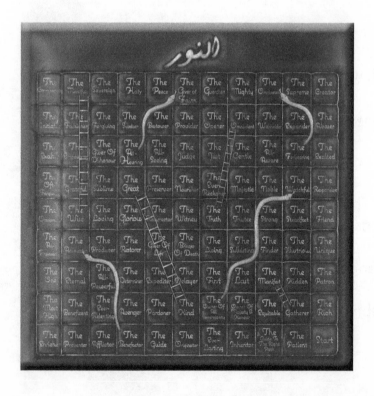

The fabric was dark blue. Square. Thick. Spongey. Yet satin-like. At the top, an Arabic word was written: *Al-Nur*. The Light.

There are ninety-nine names of God in Islam. Twenty-six of them begin with 'M'. Three begin with 'N'. To some, this says much about how the Arabic language works. To most, it says nothing.

The names were sewn into the fabric with golden thread. Each inside a box. All of them in English. Snakes and ladders slithered and stood at various angles in between. There was one dice, and three coloured stones. Şirin chose the white stone, gave the black stone to Ayşe, and to Jude, the red stone.

"I'll start."

She threw the dice. Six. She quickly moved her white stone to *The Forgiving* square.

"Why are the names of God in English?"

Ayşe smiled. Batul seemed to have fallen asleep in her lap. She gently placed the child on the bed behind her. If someone were to walk into the room at that moment and see the small collection of beings sat on the carpet, they could easily have mistaken them for a family on vacation.

Whilst it was true Ayşe was Turkish, she had been

raised in London. Her father worked as a diplomat, and for some reason, insisted they spoke only English, even at home. He also insisted his children learn Arabic. He even found them a private tutor. Deprivation and provision are so often mistaken for one another. Particularly in parenting.

"It's such a shame, I would have loved to learn Turkish. It's a genderless language. There is no distinction between 'he' and 'she'. Arabic, on the other hand, is hopelessly gendered. Hopelessly masculine, in fact."

"It is?"

"It is."

The word *Nur* is the only one of the ninety-nine names that can be used as both masculine and feminine in Arabic. Jude had never noticed this before. To imply that he had assumed the masculine was always used would be to suggest that he had ever given thought to the issue. He hadn't. To the uninterrogated mind, the masculine version was always correct.

"Only if God is really a man."

*

Jude's discomfort was uncomfortable for him. Still, he couldn't stop himself. It was one thing for Zina to reinvent Mormonism, but Ayşe's take on Islam, the Islam he had long dismissed, felt far more personal. Even threatening. For reasons he didn't fully understand.

"All of this is language, Jude. Language isn't about God. It's about us."

"This doesn't sound like a traditional Muslim position."

Ayşe was as far from being a traditional Muslim as the Dead Sea was from being sweet.

"The word 'Sufi' makes a lot of Muslim men nervous. Sufis are far too feminine to be controlled."

"But even the Quran refers to God as 'He'."

Şirin interrupted:

"We are supposed to be playing, not talking boring talk."

Ayşe threw the dice. Five. She landed on *The Wise*. A ladder was connected to this box and it carried her all the way up to *The Merciful*.

There was once a purpose for 'He'. But whatever this was, it had long been fulfilled.

"There was a time when the masculine was royal and

majestic. Now, whenever I think of men, I think of flies."

"Flies?"

"Yuck, Mother. Why are you talking about flies?"
Ayşe handed the dice to Jude. For the first time, he noticed her ring. Gold. With a small ruby. On her fourth finger.

*

In the early eighth century in the city of Basra in Iraq, a girl was born to the 'Adawiyyah family. She had three older sisters. And so, her father named her Rabi'a. The Fourth.

It was said that Rabi'a would perform a thousand ritual prostrations during the day. And a thousand at night. She was often asked why she never married. She could not bear to be distracted from God for a single moment. She said. God can provide all that men could offer.

It was said that Rabi'a was once seen running through the streets of the city with fire in one hand, and water in the other.

"What are you doing?"

They asked.

"I am going to burn paradise and douse hellfire so that both veils may be lifted from those on the quest."

She said.

*

Batul began to cry. Ayşe walked to the bed. She lay down next to her and unbuttoned her nightdress. Three deft movements with her long, slender fingers. Petals fell from the buttonholes. Jude was sure they were jasmine. *Jasminum*. She positioned her breast near the baby's mouth. Batul moved her head away, causing more petals to fall. Her crying became louder. Ayşe now uncovered both of her breasts and moved Batul nearer to her. Batul reached with her small pink hand to one breast as her lips clasped onto the other. The crying stopped. Ayşe leaned closer until her breast almost covered Batul's face. Jude soaked in the scene: Ayşe. Lying on the bed with her eyes closed. Batul. Holding onto one breast while submerged into the other. A bed of jasmine petals. Minutes passed. Against Şirin's protests, he left the room and walked to his bed. The sharp taste of the Dead Sea returned to him, the water that had entered his mouth. He was in a deep mood. When he looked in the bathroom mirror, he saw salt crystals on his eyelashes. When he finally fell asleep, he dreamt of flies.

(10)

On the best of days, Amman is a concrete jungle. An amalgamation of stone. Dust. Pigeons. And fairly recent history. Jude sat with Rami and Eman on their large balcony. Eman seemed to have a strange effect on Jude, which he did his best to ignore. Not only out of respect to his friend, but also because it made him feel emotionally vulnerable. He often found himself wanting to hold her hand as they spoke or hug her goodbye when he left. None of which he actually did. Of course.

"I don't understand. She stopped wearing her scarf on Tuesday evening?"

Jude shifted on the metal chair opposite Eman.

"And you arrived at the villa on Sunday evening?"

He straightened his cup on his saucer in front of him.

In 1990, Eman had graduated from the American University of Beirut with a degree in law, top of a class of particularly mediocre students. The development of her penchant for obscure applications of law had emerged as a salve for the burn of boredom the lecture halls had inflicted upon her. The mandatory lectures on Islamic jurisprudence were particularly tortuous. Rather than listen to the drone of her professors, Eman dove into the index of her tome-like textbooks. It was here she had found the following: in Islamic law, if a woman nurses a child who isn't her own on five separate occasions, this child becomes her son or daughter by breastfeeding.

Jude and Rami looked completely confused.

"I would guess that by Tuesday, Jude had become Ayşe's son."

*

Eman spoke as though this was a scientific fact. Jude tasted a combination of cardamom, anise, orange blossom. And milk.

"You can't be serious. I haven't even shaken her hand! Besides, I'm forty. How could any of this possibly apply to a man of my age?"

"Let's say she makes you coffee…"

"She never makes coffee. Only tea."

"Anything you can add milk to."

On Sunday, Ayşe had two daughters, and Jude had drunk one cup of tea. By Tuesday, Jude had drunk, in total, five cups of Ayşe's tea. And so now, she also had a son.

"A child by breastfeeding is no different to a real son or daughter. All the same rules apply."

To most, this rule wouldn't apply to a grown man. To some, it provided an obscure but perfectly legal way to bridge biological islands. Those who follow this opinion make reference to the position of Aisha, the Prophet's wife, who felt that this would also apply to adults. As she sat in her lecture halls, Eman had imagined the scene taking place. Adult men would partake of a drink containing a woman's breast milk, poured into a cup. Adult men breastfeeding was a vulgar, sexualised way to understand it. All it would take was a sip, on five separate occasions.

"And you become, I suppose you could say, organically connected to this woman."

*

"I'm honestly confused. Should I feel upset or privileged?"

It was immaterial, in the grand scheme of things, how Jude felt about this. It was not about how he felt. It was about how Ayşe felt. Aisha had had her own reasons for initiating this legal approach. In the year 632, the Prophet of Islam, her husband, had passed away. It was Aisha's mission to convey everything she had learnt from him to everyone who, in turn, wanted to learn it. This was her way of giving men the proximity they needed for learning to take place.

"Who knows, maybe Ayşe also wants to teach you something."

"You seem to be sympathetic to all of this?"

Eman was sympathetic to the approach. Aisha followed specific steps which she believed would lead her to a specific result. Eman tried to do the same. She applied her logic to everything, from the courtroom to the cosmos. When it came to religion, her approach was as follows: whatever you believe was there at the beginning, whether it was cosmic dust or an intelligent designer, that was, in essence, your god. If you believe we came from nothing, that was your god. Nothing.

"So, does that mean my god is a subatomic particle?"

"Do you really need me to answer that, Jude?"

*

In her waking hours, Eman was mechanically rational. In sleep, she was hopelessly lucid. That night she dreamt she was breastfeeding Jude, as Rami brushed her hair.

SEALED

(1)

Starting from his second week in Amman, Jude's days followed a very specific schedule.

Sundays: Meeting professors, staff and students.

Mondays: Meeting Salem Abdallat, the Jordanian Director of Accreditation, or 'The Fox' as Rashid referred to him.

Tuesdays: Prince Ali's literary salon.

Wednesdays: Virtual conference with LA.

Thursdays: Meeting Zina at the Ambassador's residence.

Fridays: Dead Sea trips with Ayşe and Şirin.

Saturdays: Seeking respite with Rami and Eman.

Jude Marsini tried his best to forget he was from Damascus. A place, not too far away, where people were being shot only because they believed in freedom and dignity. He deliberately didn't follow the news. And since his father had insisted he shouldn't stay in touch, the only time he truly missed anyone from back home was when Ayşe would suddenly remind him of his mother.

The connection between Ayşe and Sukayna was at first vague and intangible. But after Eman shared her breastfeeding theory, the connection became far stronger, though he never shared any of this. He had always been the listener. An apprentice of some sort. Politely learning from his teachers, though it was never clear to him what type of exotic craft they were trying to impart.

(Sunday)

Roger's printout of registered students was unhelpful.

"What exactly is a temporarily inactive student?"

Jude laid out his proposition to Walid: they would walk into each classroom and count the students themselves. Jude could not face the thought of meeting Abdallat without a clearer idea of student numbers. He, at least, needed to feel he had tried.

"This isn't a good idea, Jude. It will make everyone nervous."

The lift delivered them to the eleventh floor. Walid watched as Jude knocked on the door of the first classroom, asked permission from the professor, and proceeded to count the students. He asked if any were absent. When he was done, he scribbled a note. Minutes passed. His knuckles were millimetres from the door of the second classroom when a red-faced Abu Shanab appeared. He was out of breath and it was obvious he had run from his spot in the parking lot all the way up to the eleventh floor. Jude watched as a walrus lumbered its way towards him, down the corridor. *Odobenus rosmarus*. The walrus handed him a phone.

"I know what you were trying to do. It cannot be done

this way. You really should have listened to Walid."

"Yes, Your Excellency, I understand."

According to Nelson Sizer, famous phrenologist of the Victorian era, the intersection of ideality and acquisitiveness is located at the temples. Sitting in his office, this is exactly where Jude felt a sharp pounding. Walid tried several times to comfort him, but nothing he said was enough. It wasn't the fact that he hadn't been spoken to in such a manner since his school days. It was the sensation of blindness. More accurately the loss of sight. What he thought he'd seen was no longer there. Instead, there was darkness. And something very strange lurking within it. And as Walid had predicted, it did make everyone nervous; it even made Rashid nervous. Jude, like Abdallat before him, smelled a rat.

(Monday)

"I'm going to try to be as transparent as I can with you."

With these words, Abdallat was suddenly naked. Jude shook his head to try to get rid of this image. But Abdallat stayed stark naked. His chest hair, surprisingly, was a completely different colour to his moustache, and his calf muscles were strangely triangular.

"I tell you the number must be smaller, but you say it's better to count all kinds of categories of students to be on the safe side. I tell you, Dr. Marsini, not even an ass would accept this approach."

Jude followed the naked man into another office where various men and women were sat behind their desks. Jude was not sure whether his cheeks burned from the insult or the second-hand embarrassment he felt on account of Abdallat's sudden lack of attire.

"We will all be transparent with you, Dr. Marsini, because none of us have anything to hide."

Now everyone was naked, though some of the women remained wearing their headscarves. Headscarves on naked bodies. Jude stared hard at the floor.

The woman Abdallat introduced as Muna was asked to tell Jude what she thought of the whole situation. In a very transparent manner. Jude stared at her toes as he tried to look attentive. Her nails were painted orange.

"Dr. Abdallat, you know more than I do that this argument makes no sense at all."

Abdallat walked to another desk. A Dr. Tarek was now asked the same question. His toenails were not orange.

"I have here the applications for accreditation by seven different private universities in Jordan. Every single one of them uses every possible argument to *decrease* their numbers."

"You look unwell, Dr. Marsini."

Abdallat paused, then placed the stem of a water pipe that had suddenly appeared next to him into his mouth. He closed his eyes and inhaled deeply. He exhaled the smoke in Jude's face, and continued.

He reiterated what Dr. Tarek was saying: universities use every possible method to decrease the number of their students. It was a game both sides expected to be played.

A man entered with a tray of tea. He looked like he

was probably from Sudan. He was just as naked as everyone else. More water pipes appeared in the room.

"Have a sip, Dr. Marsini. This is very strong Jordanian tea. Perhaps it will help you see things the way we do."

(Tuesday)

In May 1919, a gathering of eighty-eight delegates took place in Damascus. The Syrian National Congress. These delegates came from Syria. Lebanon. Jordan. Palestine. They were Muslim. Christian. Jewish. They met and agreed on a constitution that was progressive, even by today's standards, and declared a constitutional monarchy with Prince Faisal as its king. This historic moment was to last only a few months. The French entered Damascus. Evicted King Faisal. And dismantled all of this in the name of a colonial mandate.

It was perhaps ironic that Jude found himself sat that afternoon with a direct descendant of King Faisal, who was asking him to share his insights into the events transpiring in Syria. Or perhaps it wasn't.

In October 2011, humanity was still harvesting the price of its failure to preserve that particular historic moment. The young men and women who flooded the news broadcasts, who marched peacefully in the name of freedom and dignity were a generation which, unlike Jude's, had had the courage to dream again. The will to envision a different future.

But their battle, once again, was with a regime which saw Syria in the same way the French mandate had once understood it: a struggle for control between different sects. An intrinsic divide between urban and rural. Orthodox and heterodox. Civilians and soldiers. Nothing could anger this type of regime more than protesters carrying slogans of unity.

"This is a battle for the soul of Syria. A battle, I fear, the regime will fight to the bitter end."

(Wednesday)

"Jude, can you explain to me again why these numbers are troubling you?"

In Jordan, as in any country Jude Marsini imagined, the head of an academic institution ought to be able to answer a very simple question: how many students are registered? Yet, for over a week he had been searching for the correct figure, which continued to elude him. The closest he had come to an answer was: somewhere between five hundred and a thousand.

"I could tell you in a matter of seconds the exact number of students we have here in LA. I've been encouraging our campuses around the world to abandon their local systems and become part of our centralized one."

Jude realised the conversation with Roger was simply going nowhere. There were no answers to be found in LA. Only more darkness. He changed the topic and asked Roger about his daughter. Apparently, she had joined the women's rowing team.

(Thursday)

"Have I told you who I'm named after?"

"No, I don't believe you have."

"Are you ready for this?"

Why he needed to be ready for something like this, Jude Marsini was unsure. But he answered with the tone of someone who fully understood that something important was about to be revealed.

"Zina Diantha Huntington Jacobs Smith Young."

Diantha was her middle name. Huntington was her maiden name. Jacobs was the surname of her first husband, Henry, from whom she was never divorced. Her second husband was Joseph, and after Joseph was killed, she was then married to Brigham Young.

Zina Diantha Huntington Jacobs Smith Young was married to Henry and Joseph. Then to Henry and Brigham.

"You mean she was Joseph's second wife, even though she was still married?"

"No. I don't mean that at all."

There was an awkward silence.

What Zina, in fact, meant was that Joseph was her second husband. Even though she was still married to her first.

There was more awkward silence.

"You see polygyny, I see polyandry."

What Zina, in fact, saw was a woman married to more than one man in nineteenth century America. And what she liked most about this was that Zina Diantha Huntington Jacobs Smith Young and Henry continued to be very close. They even had children.

"The difference, Jude, lies in where you choose to place the focus. Everyone is focused on Joseph. But Zina was way ahead of Joseph here. Joseph Smith was a prophet for his age. Zina is a prophetess for a future generation. Perhaps even for ours."

In early 1833, Joseph Smith had initiated a practice of plural marriage, through which he became sealed to multiple women. Concurrently. Either in time, or for eternity. Or for both. History struggles to document how many women were sealed, in total, to Joseph Smith. Perhaps forty. Perhaps more. It didn't matter. The only question Zina had ever asked was this: when would the moment arrive for a woman to do this? Or more precisely, when would a woman seize the reigns of history and harness this practice as a portal to the divine? Polygyny. Polyandry. Plural marriages. None of these terms meant anything. Seeing through sealing. The beauty of God, through beautiful men. This is what Zina wanted.

"Lower your head, Jude Marsini."

*

Male honeybees, *Apis mellifera*, are known as drones. Their sole purpose is to mate with the queen. The act occurs in mid-air. The drone climaxes with such force that he explodes. This process is often audible to the human ear. It makes a popping sound. The drone's endophallus is ruptured and remains inside the queen. The drone dies. The entire process lasts less than five seconds.

*

Jude looked straight into Zina's eyes. His mother once described in detail why the eyes of Elizabeth Taylor were different. Blue, in its various shades, is common. She explained. Elizabeth Taylor's were not blue. Hers were a deep violet. Zina's eyes, at least on this particular evening, seemed violet too. Jude Marsini decided, right there and then, that he would comply. He would do so not for Rashid's sake. Not because he wanted to keep his job. Not because he wanted to stay out of Syria. He would comply because these were the eyes of a woman no one should say no to.

Zina placed her outstretched hand over his head. As a monarch would with a sword. Or as a prophet would to confer a blessing.

"By virtue of the holy priesthood and the authority vested in me, I pronounce you, Jude Marsini, mine for time and for all eternity. I seal upon you the blessings of the holy resurrection, with power to come forth in the morning of the first resurrection, clothed in glory, immortality, and eternal life."

Jude felt a sudden warm flash. He reached to Zina's hand, as though he was afraid that he was about to fall.

"Close your eyes."

This time, her lips arrived first. Pressed against his. He smelled white musk. Seconds passed. The lips touched his chin. His neck. His chest. His stomach. She unbuckled his belt. The Calvin Klein boxers he had become attached to ever since coming across a large billboard in Princeton, the boxers he had so far never removed in the presence of another man or woman, were slipped quickly over his hips. Jude Marsini was a virgin, a fact he didn't enjoy thinking about. He felt her fingers on his skin. They were remarkably warm. Her ring was remarkably cold. He noticed she wore it on her index finger. The stone was violet.

*

Jude wondered why now, of all times, he was thinking of his mother. Why Zina's presence had summoned her memory. What was it about her? About them? Perhaps it was their shared indifference. Their effortless dismissal of male authority. Their natural claim to female sovereignty. The ancestral feminine. The power they called upon from an age when the only gods were goddesses.

*

Jude still hadn't realised he was fully erect. He was not to realise this until her lips made contact with him. She kissed him gently. No one had ever done this to him. Never had he allowed such an image to even cross his mind. He felt both of her hands on his lower back. Then he felt her take him in fully. His body jerked. Her lips tightened around him. Everything that flowed out of him remained inside of her. Jude thought about drone bees. Zina waited until the tension in his body eased, then she raised herself towards him. The first thing she noticed were his eyes. Wet with tears. The first thing he noticed was the small white butterfly. *Pieris rapae*. Resting on her lip.

*

After dinner, Şirin had forgone her usual night-time ritual of reading on Jude's bed. Instead, she had requested that he tell her a story. He tried. But all he could think of was butterflies.

"You're really not very good at this, Doctor."

"I guess story telling isn't one of my best talents."

"Well then, someone else will have to tell one."

Şirin ran out of the room, returning a few moments later. She sat cross-legged on the bed before Jude, holding out her fist. She stuck up her thumb. On it, she had drawn a face. Elaborate. With eyelashes. In different colours.

"Say hello to Binan. That's what my baby sister should have been called. She's the princess of storytelling. Are you ready?"

There once was a white rabbit named Kusa, and she was having a picnic with her friends. But her friends were all so very boring. All they wanted to talk about was grass and carrots. So, Kusa decided she would go exploring. Suddenly, she saw a young human girl who was wearing glittery shoes. The little girl was walking towards her home. Kusa couldn't take her eyes off the glittery shoes, the way they sparkled in the sunlight. And so, she followed the little girl, all the way home. Just before she closed the door, Kusa raced inside and found herself for the first time in a human house. It was big, and dark, and the floors were slippery. Now, Kusa felt very scared. She felt trapped. She crept through the house, until she found some stairs. She scurried, up and up, until she reached a hallway. It looked so long, and there were so many doors. One of them was open. In a panic, Kusa scuttled inside and hid under the bed.

"But guess what she found under the bed?"

"What?"

Şirin rolled her eyes, and wiggled her thumb.

"It's a *re-to-i-kal* question. You're not supposed to say *what*."

Under the bed, Kusa looked around. She wasn't alone. All around her were other rabbits. So many white rabbits. She even recognised one of them.

"Aunt Lusa? We thought you were dead."

Aunt Lusa wasn't dead. She was here for exactly the same reason as Kusa. The glittery shoes. And, like Kusa, she was stuck. They would probably all die of starvation.

"But why don't you try to escape?"

They couldn't escape because the young girl had

a very dangerous brother. A brother who enjoyed scaring the rabbits to death every time he came into the room. As Aunt Lusa said this, a young boy walked in.

"Who's under the bed today I wonder? Smells like rabbit stew to me!"

"Şirin, that's cruel."

Şirin placed a finger on her lips. Jude wasn't sure if she were signalling to him or the rabbits to remain quiet. Her thumb returned to its story-telling position.

A few moments later, the girl with glittery shoes walked in. She told her brother to leave. She took off her shoes and then got on top of the bed. She yawned once or twice, and then fell asleep. Kusa hopped gently until she was in the middle of the room. She saw that there was a window and that it was open. Then, she went back under the bed. She had a plan.

"We are going to jump out of the window. We are not going to become rabbit stew."

The rabbits thought she had lost her mind. They couldn't fly. They weren't birds.

But Kusa's mother had taught her a special prayer. It would get them all out of there alive. All they had to do was trust it. Trust it with all their hearts. If they did, they would dine on carrots that night. If they didn't, the boy would dine on rabbit stew. The rabbits stared at each other and ground their teeth.

"Just make sure you truly trust it with all your heart, or it won't work."

Kusa said the prayer out loud, and then she gathered all her courage and hopped quietly to the window. And she jumped. The moment she did, a strong gust of wind arrived and carried her safely to the ground. The other rabbits followed her. One by one, they would close their eyes and say: "We trust the prayer." And then they would jump. One by one, they landed safely on the grass. All but one. He decided he just couldn't leave without one of the glittery shoes. Rabbits, you must know, are crazy like that. He tried lifting the shoe with his mouth and was happy to see that it wasn't heavy at all. He hopped with the shoe between his teeth over to the window. But because he was so distracted with the shoe, you see, he forgot to close his eyes and trust the prayer.

And so, when he jumped, the wind didn't arrive. And the girl and her family had delicious rabbit stew for dinner. The end.

Şirin tucked her thumb into her fist, as though putting Binan to bed.

"Mother says sad endings protect us from bad beginnings. Good night, Doctor."

*

Captain D'Arpentigny was once asked how he had discovered his system of determining a person's character and mental condition from a glance at their hands.

"By a divine inspiration."

He said.

In Sukayna's library, Jude had found D'Arpentigny's book, *The Science of the Hand*, replete with its theories, diagrams, and quotations by Persian poets and philosophers. The work was Victorian. Translated into English in 1889.

It was said that the shape of a person's hand belied their sensibilities. It was also said that one could tell whether a person was governed by their heart or their head by the size of their thumb.

"In the absence of any other proofs, the thumb would convince me of the existence of God."

Isaac Newton said.

(Friday)

Daylight hours at the Dead Sea always followed a familiar pattern. The buffet with Şirin. Ice cream. Swimming. The evening game of Snakes and Ladders. At night, nothing was planned.

Jude Marsini slept in a room adjoined to that of Ayşe and her daughters. The door connecting the two was open. It was through this door that Jude, on his return from the bathroom, noticed Ayşe, awake, sitting on a prayer carpet. She seemed to have just finished praying. He paused for a second and was about to apologise when he heard her say:

"Come."

Ayşe gestured for him to sit next to her. The prayer mat was green and gold. Jude noticed small blue flowers scattered across it. *Myosotis*. Forget-me-nots. She guided his head towards her lap. He curled his knees and slid his hands between his thighs. One of her hands was on his shoulder. The other on his forehead. At the intersection of human nature and benevolence. If Nelson Sizer had been correct.

"I never shared with you how my husband died."

Though the sensation of her hand on his head had lulled Jude into an almost hypnotic state, he kept his eyes open. He wanted to stay alert. Focused. If for nothing more than to prove he was worthy of the secret she was about to share.

On the 19th of April 1997, Ayşe had taken an oath, in the bathroom mirror, that she would marry only for love. On the 19th of April 2003, she had met Riyad, whilst working as a flight attendant. It felt right to fall in love thirty thousand feet above the ground. She trusted her heart more when she was so far up in the air. At first, it was beautiful. Her body had opened to him. He had made a home inside her. Then a child. When Şirin was born, Riyad began to change. Women throughout history have wondered what it is about men that makes them show their worst when they are needed the most. How they fail to realise how a woman, a mother, feels when the man with whom she has made a home acts unkindly because he feels he is now sexually unfulfilled. Through the fabric of his shirt Jude could feel the warmth of Ayşe's fingers.

They had been living in Germany at the time. Riyad was of Lebanese descent but had been born and raised in Germany. Rashid had found him and asked him to come and work for him, so they moved first to Beirut, and later to Amman. Jordan brought out the worst in Riyad. One night, he returned and confessed to his wife that he'd had a brief affair. An Eastern European waitress he met somewhere. He couldn't even pronounce her name correctly. Ayşe hadn't been paying enough attention to him. He said. That was why it happened. He said. As he shared this with his wife, she felt her body close. Like a flower folding in on itself, aware that the sun had set. Still, Riyad would try. And try. But it would have been easier for him to make love to a wall than it was for him to make love to his wife again. Years passed. They lived in the same home, but they lived separate lives. Every now and then, Riyad would gather his energy and try again. He would start with roses. Gifts. But nothing he did helped. Ayşe could not forgive him.

"Betrayal isn't really the right word. It feels too masculine. You let someone inside you, and they turn around and tell you they were inside someone else."

One night, Riyad came back home, and walked straight into Ayşe's bedroom. He held her down and pushed. It was no use. He left to the kitchen and came back with a bottle of olive oil. It was green, and made of glass. The branch on the label had three black olives on it. The bottle was full. He poured the oil over her. And over himself. Then he pushed again. He held the brass rods behind his wife's head and pushed. He pushed with all his force, and she felt him enter. Seconds passed. Riyad's body collapsed over her. That was the night Batul was conceived.

"That was the night he died."

*

Ayşe pulled Jude against her, and leaned over him. Her arms enveloped him. He felt the fabric of her nightdress on his cheek. The soft fullness of her breasts against him. And from deep within, the beating of her heart. He could smell cardamom. Anise. Orange blossom.

Ayşe hadn't moved when Riyad collapsed. She knew something had gone wrong, but she felt the right thing to do was to honour the silence, in silence. Hours passed. When suddenly, she felt a presence. It wasn't his. It felt like an invitation. A gentle shower of light, arriving from elsewhere. Then it spoke.

"What did it say?"

"Come."

"Come? Come where?"

"It just said come."

"But where did it take you?"

"To a place where men are not welcome."

"Not even me?"

"Not even you."

*

In 1774, Ann Lee crossed the Atlantic from England to America. She took with her a small band of followers. None of her children were amongst them. All had died in infancy. Soon after their arrival in America, her husband deserted her. Ann Lee's followers came to believe that she embodied the perfections of God in female form. She advocated male and female equality. And celibacy.

"Put your hands to work, and your hearts to God."

Said Mother Ann.

"Come."

She said.

*

Come Pretty Love

Oh my pretty Mother's home,
Sweeter than the honey in the comb.

Oh my pretty Mother's home,
Sweeter than the honey in the comb.

Come, come pretty love, come, come, come,
Come, come pretty love, I want some.

Shaker "Gift" song received by Patsy Williamson

(Saturday)

Eman seemed exceptionally beautiful that morning. She was wearing a halter neck. Light blue. Long. And white sandals. The clasps at her ankles were gold.

"Eman, I have another riddle for you. This one is numerical."

Eman was familiar with the explanation Jude shared about the requirements for accreditation. The ratio of students to professors.

"Well, you see the problem is most universities usually try to reduce the number of their actual students, so they don't have to hire so many professors. In our case, we seem to be inflating the number."

"That's strange."

Jude told Eman of his search for an answer to the question of student numbers at the ACA. How no one seemed to have an explanation for why records showed a thousand students when in actuality they probably had closer to five hundred. He told her how every time he tried to identify the exact number, it seemed everyone was conspiring to stop him.

"It must be income."

"Income?"

"It must be."

If an institution has a thousand students, then they make a million dollars a semester. For example. If they have only half that amount, they would probably be making something closer to five hundred thousand.

"Someone wants it to seem like you are making a million. Who hires the professors at ACA?"

The main branch in LA was responsible for all academic expenses, including professors. Rashid, on the other hand, took care of the premises, infrastructure, and the networks required to keep the place legal.

"But what possible advantage would he gain from inflating the number of students if no real income is made through this?"

Eman needed more time to think. She assigned Jude the task of finding out whether Rashid had any other businesses. Jude made a mental note of this, which he filed, unbeknownst to himself, next to gold ankle straps, and the dust of Jordanian Octobers.

"Give me a call when you find something. You do know my number?"

This took Jude by surprise. He glanced at Rami as though to check whether he was uncomfortable with the idea of his having direct contact with his wife that didn't include him. But Rami was staring at his phone, surrounded by a thin film of cigarette smoke, totally indifferent to what Eman had proposed. Jude wrote down the digits she dictated to him.

"I'm grateful for your help with this. I hate to admit it, but I'm a little scared. Though I'm not even sure what it is that I'm scared of."

"It's those types of fears that play with us the most."

BAPTISED

(1)

In the third week of October, Rashid asked Jude to schedule an 'intersession' during the forthcoming vacation—a period during which students had the option to take special courses that they could complete in only ten days. They would attend a four-hour class every day and were expected to digest information that normally took at least three months to learn. Jude saw this as another vulgar example of how commercial higher education had become. It was as he was planning these courses in his office with Walid that he received a phone call from a person he had not heard from since he left Damascus: Abu Ammar.

"Dr. Marsini, I have something for you from your father."

They met in Abdali, where the taxis arriving from and departing to Damascus gathered. Abu Ammar seemed tired and pale.

The Damascus Jude Marsini left had changed. Abu Ammar didn't leave his home after dark. No one did. Abu Ammar was an Alawite, a servant of the Prince of the Bees. But he was born in Damascus. Damascus was his home. Now all his friends and neighbours talked about was leaving. They said their children would never be safe if the army kept attacking Sunnis.

Abu Ammar's cousin was an officer. He swore it was the Sunnis who were shooting at them. Abu Ammar was too old for this.

"Whatever you do, do not come back now."

From his pocket, Abu Ammar drew a key. The key that Jude's father had asked him to give to his son. Jude's father was a wise man. He hadn't wanted Abu Ammar to put it in an envelope because he said the border guards might find it and think it was suspicious.

"I said to him, who would dare search Abu Ammar?"

He had also sent a note. He said that Abu Ammar should tell Jude that this contained the address of the house to which the key belonged. An Italian marble client who owed him had arranged for it to be transferred to his name. Or Jude's name. Abu Ammar wasn't sure. Jude studied the card. It was his father's handwriting. He knew it well.

Via Campo delle Monache, 33 Sperlonga

Jude's father would be happy to hear that his son was doing well. But he wanted him to have options. Just in case. Jude's father was a wise man.

"I must leave now."

A day had arrived when even the servant of the Prince

of the Bees would rather be home before sunset.

(2)

When Jude proposed that they take a break from the insanity of intersession and find something for lunch, he knew Walid would agree. As formal as Walid was, he could not resist an invitation to eat. Jude needed an informal setting, and an absence of blinking red lights, to carry out the task Eman had given him. He didn't know how much Walid knew about Rashid's business affairs, but he was certain he knew far more than he did.

Lunch was carnivorous. Meat of various shapes and shades. It seemed a fitting match for Jude's hunt for information. It took less than an hour for Jude to learn that Rashid was far more naïve than he had expected him to be. As far as Walid knew, Rashid was only involved in education. The ACA and three high schools in Beirut. The Lebanese accountants of the ACA were the real managers of the place and were almost certainly connected to a very powerful political party in Lebanon. Of this, Walid was convinced.

"He doesn't just trust them, he empowers them. Remember that day when you were stopped from your counting tour?"

The tour had been stopped by Osama. The Chief Accountant. All he had had to do was phone Rashid and inform him that Jude's little investigation wasn't in the institution's best interests.

"I've said too much."

Walid was usually more careful. He had made a career out of bureaucratic tight-rope walking. But he liked Jude Marsini. He wasn't what he had expected him to be. He was honest. Naïve.

"Perhaps that's why Rashid likes you. You remind him of himself."

The thought of seeing Eman on her own was too powerful for Jude to allow himself to interact with it. The coffee shop she had specified for their meeting was not too far from Wild Jordan. She was dressed in a grey suit. Her hair was carefully combed back. For the first time since he had met her, Jude felt he had understood why he found her beautiful in the way he did. He watched the condensation trickle down the side of his pomegranate juice. He didn't speak until all the ice cubes in his glass had melted.

Eman's initial theory was this: Rashid must have income from somewhere else which wasn't quite as clean as income from a branch of an American university. The artificial inflation of numbers of students allowed him to incorporate funds from other sources without it being noticed. Other sources. Shady sources.

The problem with the theory was this: if Rashid was engaged in such activities, he would then have to share a percentage of it with the main branch in LA. He couldn't share dubiously sourced funds with the head office.

Eman explained: under the cover of additional student fees, the money would come out clean. Rashid's share would also appear entirely legitimate.

Income from an academic institution. Nothing more. One problem remained: either Rashid was as naïve as Walid believed Jude to be, and he let his accountants run the place, simply taking home his pay cheque with no questions asked. Or, he wasn't, and he complied because he had to. Given Eman's experience with the darker side of the Levantine legal system, the latter seemed more likely.

"You mean his accountant is a front for some powerful figure in Lebanon?"

Either way, this meant that Jude Marsini happened to be the dean of the largest money laundering operation in Amman.

*

Eman asked for the cheque and paid the bill. She walked out and followed a side road that led to some stone steps. They seemed to spiral down. Endlessly. The entire area seemed void of people. As though it had been cleared just for them. Jude followed Eman down the steps. They seemed to become steeper. She reached to his hand. He held tightly to hers. Halfway down, she stopped. She placed what seemed to be a handkerchief on the floor and sat. She was still holding his hand. Jude made no effort to pull it away. This was so distant from his interactions with Ayşe and Zina. So normal. Perhaps this was what attracted him to the wife of his apparently indifferent friend.

"Now that I've solved your riddles, Jude, you have to help me solve mine."

Her eyes were dark brown, and felt like black holes pulling him in. The grey of her suit blended into the stone of the steps. Jude wasn't sure where his surroundings ended and Eman began.

"You're the only riddle I can't seem to crack."

Sperlonga is a beach town approximately halfway between Rome and Naples. It was once inhabited by Emperor Tiberius. Jude told Eman that his father had purchased a villa there and that the key to this place had been delivered to him. Eman removed her black leather shoes and stretched out her feet onto the lower steps. Jude counted each of her toes. Like a nurse, dutifully declaring a newly born child to be perfect. Ten toes. No butterflies. No petals. Eman was always Eman.

Jude's phone was set to make a distinct sound when Adel sent a message. Jude recognised the tone instantly as it beeped. He wasn't sure if he was grateful.

You are wanted at the Ambassador's residence. Let me know where you are, so I can pick you up and drive you there.

Jude paused for a second, then typed back:
I will take a taxi there. I'll let you know when I'm done.

"You're leaving?"

*

Jude collapsed on the back seat of the taxi. The inside of his eyelids replayed the scene of Eman. Sitting on the steps. The taxi reeked with the smell of old tobacco. The highway outside the taxi turned into a canyon floor. The buildings on either side that flew by walled him in. He opened the window to let in some air. It only served to suffocate him further. His phone rang. It was Rami:

"Did Eman break the news?"

"News?"

"She said she planned on sharing it with you today. We've separated, Jude, we are now legally divorced. We finalised the paperwork yesterday."

It was what they wanted.

They said.

They weren't fighting. They didn't hate each other. Rami wanted children. That was all.

He said.

The older he got, the worse it got.

She said.

They considered adoption. But it wasn't what they wanted.

He said.

It just wasn't the same. They just weren't the same.

They said.

*

Jude was upset. Zina was not supposed to be part of his Mondays. He suspected that whatever it was she wanted had nothing to do with the ACA.

"Madam is downstairs in the spa. Follow me, please."

Even as his anger ricocheted around his head, he felt his body beginning to react to the thought of seeing Zina.

"What took you so long?"

The basement of the residence was large. It seemed to be a complete sports facility. There was a jacuzzi.

A sauna. Various types of treadmills. Bicycles. Numerous exercise machines designed to elicit innumerable forms of exertion.

The woman who had been waiting for him was wearing a short white robe. She had a towel wrapped around her head. On her shoulder sat an *Ornithoptera alexandrae*. Queen Alexandra's birdwing. The creature's wings, the largest of any butterfly in the world, opened and closed. Opened and closed. Meditatively.

"Well, someone deserves to be fired for this. Maybe we should fire you. Or better yet, let's fire that man-for-all-seasons Rashid calls a driver."

Jude tried to exhale. She clearly knew a lot about the ACA, though she was never interested in talking about it.

"I've been having this feeling of intensity for the past few days."

"Intensity?"

It was very spiritual. She claimed. This intensity. Like someone, or something, was trying to reveal itself to her. She had needed a scribe. She had summoned Jude Marsini.

"Scribe?"

An explanation would have bored both of them. More Zina than Jude, in truth.

"Just take your clothes off. There's a towel hanging behind you if you're feeling modest."

She stood by the door of the sauna and stared at him. He stared back at her. Violet eyes. That no one could say no to.

In the basement of the American Ambassador's residence in Amman, Jordan, Jude Marsini removed his clothes. He was far too embarrassed for a towel to salvage any of his modesty. It remained hanging on the hook. Zina handed him a large notebook and a black pen. The paper was waterproof. The birdwing danced away through the air.

Zina took off her robe and threw it on the bench. She resembled a Capitoline Venus. Her hand seemed to be deliberately blocking the blonde fuzz between her legs. Her body was toned. The freckles he had seen splashed across her shoulders spread down her back. Her nails were painted a pale pink. There was a small scar above her left knee. Jude felt pins and needles on the inside and outside of his skin. It might have been the heat.

He noticed Zina was holding a stone with her right hand. A small brown coloured stone. It looked like a dormouse curled up in her palm.

In 1829, over a period of sixty-five days, from the 7th of April until the 30th of June, Joseph Smith translated the Book of Mormon from golden plates. He wore a hat which he would pull down over his face. Inside the hat was a stone. The 'Seer Stone'. Small. Brown coloured.

Once, Martin Harris, his scribe, replaced the stone in Joseph's hat. To test him.

"All is as dark as Egypt."

He said.

*

Zina unwrapped the towel from her head and covered her face. She leant back against the sauna wall. She slipped her hand, and the stone, beneath the towel. Her voice arrived like a Gregorian chant. Deep and melodious:

"Only Corianton,
Not Alma,
Only Corianton became a child of mine.
I had placed my word in the land of Siron,
My throne descended on the home of Isabel,
My light brushed against her hair,
My rain fell upon her shoulders.
To the hardened, she was a harlot,
Yet to me, she was why

Why I sailed through Lehi
Why I wrote through Moroni
Why I loved through Joseph
And why I returned in the latter time.
But it was only Corianton,
Only Corianton who recognized my sign."

She removed the towel. Her skin was deep red. Wet with sweat.

"Now, write below: The Plates of Isabel."

Jude focused. His eyes had never been this hot. His eyelids scratched against them. His bones seemed to be crying out to be released from their blanket of flesh.

Zina exhaled. As though relieved of a heavy burden she had been carrying.

"Who exactly is Corianton?"

Corianton was the son of a prophet named Alma. The Book of Mormon relates that he was seduced by a harlot named Isabel. History now holds that he was the only one in his generation to recognise Isabel for what she really was.

Jude wiped the sweat from his face and struggled to stay composed.

She was a sign. She said. Of God. Disguised as a prostitute.

"Don't you love how God shatters our expectations?"

*

Zina climbed down from her bench. Jude could tell that his body was no longer under his control. It reacted to her regardless of how much his mind might object. He watched as Zina lowered her head into his lap. Her mouth had moved from reciting ancient and scared hymns to doing those things that made him feel watermelons breaking against his head. Lemons exploding in his mouth. Sharp objects racing down his skin. Minutes passed. She raised her face and looked into his eyes.

Jude Marsini knew that if he didn't leave the sauna that instant, he would most certainly die.

"But wouldn't it be beautiful for you to die like this?"

*

"These particular mussels will leave you wanting to go back to the sauna you were dying to escape."

"It was dying that I was trying to escape."

The mussels had arrived in a few minutes; it was

clear that it had all been pre-planned. They seemed like precious dark stones. Adorned with lemon zest. Parsley. Dill. Thyme. They sat at the table. Jude was more thirsty than hungry. He gulped down his sparkling water and poured more. Zina was very particular about everything. Including eating etiquettes. She would hold the mussel with one hand and use a special fork to extract the meat. She would dip her fork in garlic sauce and eat the mussel in one bite. The empty shell was placed carefully in a bowl. A smile would follow. Jude tried to copy her. He lost count of how many he ate.

Zina knew all about Jude's Dead Sea trips. With his girls. As she called them. Her proposal would complement this. She would send a car to the Movenpick. The place she wanted to take him was just a short trip from the hotel. She promised she wouldn't keep him long.

Jude realised his shell bowl was overflowing. He knew it was time to leave. Zina surveyed the room swiftly. Then kissed him on the ear.

"Friday."

She whispered.

(4)

Jude would try the jacuzzi for the first time since arriving in Amman. He poured several bath lotions from bottles that he had not bothered earlier to check. Lavender. Citrus. Peppermint. By the time he got into the water, it was covered with white mountains, hills and valleys. He carried some of the foam to his nose and inhaled the strong scents. He wanted to be back with Eman. Right where he had left her on the steps. He wanted to finish the scene Zina interrupted. There was something about Eman that was calming in ways no one else could compete with. She could make him forget, for a short while at least, that he was from Syria. Or that the Syrians he loved were being hunted like animals by vicious security officers. He imagined her completing her question. He imagined her asking him if he felt something towards her. He saw her remove her shoes and gesture for him to follow her. She danced her way down the steps, all the way down to a shop that sold *kanafeh*. Pastry layered with white cheese. Drenched in syrup. Served hot. She ordered two cups of Arabic coffee. And they sat around a small table and ate and drank. He could taste the rosewater in his mouth. Fragrant. Then the coffee. Bitter. A scene that included everything he needed to erase Zina and her mussels.

(5)

"Mother would not approve of this."

Jude woke up to a goldfinch peeking into the bathroom. He had fallen asleep in the bathtub.

A little before nine, he arrived at Abdallat's office. His meeting had been postponed from Monday. Jude smelled of peppermint.

The man Abdallat introduced as Dr. Fayez was old. Tired. Kind. The large conference table stretched out like a pool of quicksand between them. Jude took a seat, placing his hands in his lap. They had asked him there today because they felt he was different.

"Different?"

In a positive sense. Different because Jude was not part of what was going on, though at times he had been guilty of trying to defend it. Jude felt like a teenager would when his parents finally had conclusive proof that he smoked. That all his past creative excuses would not help him this time. The quicksand shifted.

The ACA, of which he was the dean, the highest academic authority, was engaged in illegal activities. Dr. Fayez placed his hands on the table and lent forward. Jude watched them disappear into the sand.

"Money laundering. It's that simple. We don't have all the information yet. But we will soon. Once we do, everyone involved, especially those with important positions…"

"Like yourself…"

Abdallat interjected.

"… Will be the first to be held accountable."

But they had asked him there today because they felt he was different. And it was because he was different that they wanted him to help clear up this mess. In return: clemency.

Jude was silent. There was nothing really left to add. He was expected to surrender. He decided he would. At the very least so he could leave and contact Rashid to figure out what must be done.

"The files, Dr. Marsini, we need the files. You need to look in the basement."

"The basement?"

All the important documents were in the office of the Chief Accountant. Mr. Osama Raad. Jude had not met him. This is why Jude was different. He was the Dean of the ACA and he had not yet met the Chief Accountant. But even if he had, Jude did not see how he could possibly obtain the files. The real files.

"This is where your Princeton education should prove helpful."

"I wasn't taught to break into offices at Princeton."

Abdallat and Fayez laughed.

Jude stared at them. They were both now dressed in police uniforms. They had come to make an arrest and had agreed to postpone it only if he agreed to cooperate. They signed their names on his release form.

*

Tuesdays were designated for Prince Ali's literary salon. Jude told Adel it was cancelled. He informed Walid that he would take advantage of his free evening to stay in the office and work on intersession files, in the company of the red blinking light. As the last of the staff were leaving, Rashid phoned:

"How was your meeting today with The Fox?"

"It was the same as usual, Your Excellency."

Rashid was in Mecca, performing the pilgrimage. Jude found the image of Marlon Brando in white robes unnerving. Rashid had received a message from the Ministry. He said. He was concerned.

"You never know what to take seriously. This is why I have you."

"Yes, Your Excellency. I would, of course, let you know immediately if there was anything to be concerned about."

Jude stared out of his window. His mind had made the decision on his behalf not to share with Rashid what had transpired earlier that day. He had formally joined the team of The Fox. *Vulpes*.

*

Night fell. The building seemed empty. He could see Abu Shanab standing near his small room in the parking lot. He wondered how long walruses could last without water. His eyes flicked from the moustache to the camera in the corner of the parking lot. The small black spider-like contraption. With spider siblings in every office. But, if Rashid was in Mecca, then he could not be watching. Perhaps this was exactly the opportunity he needed.

He took the lift to the ground floor.

Jude prepared forty-seven things to say in case someone met him.

He took the stairs from the ground floor to the basement.

He added five excuses to his list.

There was only one office. The lights were turned off, though a small window near the ceiling brought in enough light for Jude to walk around the place without bumping into anything. All he wanted was one file. A file that had numbers. The numbers he had searched for in vain since he first arrived.

The entirety of the office was grey. There might have been five filing cabinets. There might have been twelve. Jude saw thirty-nine.

His mother used to share stories about how a person could focus all their mental energy on something and almost wish it into being. He opened the first drawer. The second drawer. The third. His wishing wasn't working. A guard dog padded its way into the room. Snarling.

Seconds passed. Next filing cabinet. First drawer. Another guard dog appeared. The growling grew louder. Jude sifted through folders. The noise attracted more dogs. Second drawer. Third drawer. Nine dogs. German shepherds. *Canis lupus familiaris.*

Third cabinet. First drawer. Fourth folder: *Registered students: Fall 2011*. Twelve dogs.

This was it. He had found what he was looking for. Jude's heart beat faster. There was no time to think about consequences. It was too late for that. He slid the file inside his jacket. The dogs snapped at his ankles. They followed him out of the room before he could close the door on them. They ran up the stairs behind him, still snarling. He managed to pull the staircase door shut loudly before they got through.

He frantically pressed the button for the lift.

3

2

1

The doors opened slowly. To reveal Abu Shanab. He stared at Jude. His moustache twitched. Jude smelled sea salt. And shellfish. Each and every one of his fifty-two excuses evaporated. He smiled, stepped inside, and pressed the button for the twelfth floor. He stayed as silent as Abu Shanab.

Abu Shanab got out on the fifth floor. Jude felt lightheaded. Possibly because he had not yet exhaled. In his office, he used his phone to take pictures of every single document in the folder. There were sixty-three documents. It took eight minutes.

Jude wondered whether this was really the right moment to place the folder back in the office. The assumption that he had a choice was a false one. He knew he could not possibly sleep that night, or any other night, without having placed it back where it belonged.

He walked back to the lift.

12
11
10
9
8
7
6
5
4
3
2
1

The dogs were still in the stairwell. They snapped at his ankles. He saw pools of their saliva on the floor. Jude found the third cabinet. He slipped the folder back in its place. He climbed back up the stairs. The dogs had fallen asleep.

(6)

Jude Marsini woke to the voice of Ayşe.

"You should take these pills; they will bring the fever down."

The word 'flu' is derived from the Medieval Latin term *influentia*, meaning 'influence'. Centuries ago, the effects of the flu were thought to be influenced by the stars. By the time Jude had arrived home, his entire body ached. His head pounded. He had been shivering. He had cocooned himself in bed. Still wearing his shoes. All he could see were stars.

He swallowed the pills and went back to sleep.

(7)

Jude decided he would not swim in the Dead Sea. He had recovered, but still felt fragile. He sat next to Ayşe on the shore and watched Şirin practice her floating. Batul slept beside them.

My driver will be at your hotel in fifteen minutes. Bring something extra to wear with you.

Until that moment, Zina had become a figment of Jude's imagination. He explained to Ayşe that an officer from the American embassy wanted to see him for coffee, and that he would return very soon. And as he walked out of the lobby with his bag, he realised just how easy it had become for him to skew the truth. The survivalist Damascene genes were a part of his DNA after all. His father would be proud.

*

On the banks of the River Jordan, at a place now known as Bethany, Jesus approached John the Baptist, and asked to be baptised. It was the fifteenth year of the rein of Tiberius. Jesus was approximately thirty years old. John tried to convince his cousin otherwise.

"In this way we will do all that God requires."

He said.

John agreed.

On the banks of the Susquehanna River, at a place known as Harmony, Pennsylvania, Joseph Smith and Oliver Cowdery, his scribe, baptised each other. It was the 15th of May 1829. For most Mormons, baptism is essential to entering the Kingdom of God. For some, this opportunity does not end with death. The deceased have a final chance to gain access to the Celestial Kingdom. By being baptised. Vicariously.

*

Jude found a white jeep waiting outside the hotel, and a smiling driver gesturing for him to get in.

"Where are we going?"

"To Bethany, sir."

When the jeep parked, he found Zina standing in a white robe. Longer than the one she had worn at the sauna. But confusing, nevertheless.

He followed her. The place was empty. Emptied. Perhaps deliberately for the wife of the Ambassador. There were two men walking a few meters behind them, the driver and a bodyguard.

The Jordan River where John baptised Christ may have once been majestic. Today, it is a brownish-green stream of water. On its east bank lies the Hashemite Kingdom of Jordan. Its west bank is in the State of Israel. Jordanian army officers with stern faces paced up and down the east bank. Israeli officers paced the west. Wooden steps lead down to the water.

"We have the place all to ourselves. But only until noon. Come, let's go in."

She dropped her robe to the ground. Jude was relieved to see that she had on a white bathing suit underneath it. But he had no plans to follow her into the water. He hadn't been willing to swim in the pure Dead Sea that morning. He was adamant he would not be swimming in this muddy stream. Zina ignored his hesitation. Reluctance. Discomfort. He explained he hadn't been well all week. That the water really didn't look clean.

"This water is the plasma of life. You would drink it if you knew what it contained. It doesn't look clean on purpose to discourage tourists and amateurs. Spiritual tourists and amateurs."

Her words didn't help, but he followed her down the steps. He decided he was not going to undress in front of Jordanian soldiers. He left his jacket on the railing. His shoes and socks on the wooden platform.

The water felt warm and murky. He felt the silt between his toes. The brown liquid rose over his navel. He tried to keep his eyes fixed on the space between Zina's shoulder blades. He blinked. The whole stream was full of women who looked exactly like her. They were all staring at him. All making sure he didn't try to escape.

Zina positioned Jude in front of her. She placed her right hand in the air, as though facing the heavens. Her left hand held his against his chest.

"Jude Marsini, having been commissioned by Jesus Christ, I baptize you in the name of the Father, and of the Son, and of the Holy Ghost. Amen."
She pulled him into the water. Jude felt the taste of mud in his mouth. She pulled him out again. Quickly.

He blinked. There was only one Zina. Her face radiating like he had never seen it before. Though he felt wet, dirty, and convinced he had again been afflicted with the flu, and probably much worse, he didn't say a word.

It is said that when the Israelites escaped from Egypt, Miriam took a tambourine in her hand. All the women followed her, and they began to dance.

It is said that Rumi was once walking through the market in Konya when he heard the beating of coppersmiths. Enraptured by the rhythm, Rumi raised his hand to the sky. And as he repeated the name of God, he began to dance.

It is said that Mother Ann and her followers crossed the Atlantic in a ship named Mariah. Aboard the ship, they began to dance. The captain threatened to throw them overboard. They continued their worship. It is better to listen to God than a man. Mother Ann said. A storm struck. It will sink the ship. They said. God will not condemn it while we are in it. She said. The ship was saved. They continued to dance.

*

When he finally arrived back at the room in the Movenpick, Jude heard music. In his room, he found Ayşe and Şirin dancing to *La Macarena*. The volume was loud. Even Batul seemed to be smiling and trying to move her small body.

"Dance with us, Doctor."

So, he did. With his girls. As Zina called them.

They sang Ayşe's lyrics to the nineties hit tune:

"Shake away your sins and you'll be holy,
Shake away your sins and you'll be holy,
Shake away your sins and you'll see the glory,
Shake away your sins."

They sang. And danced. Until they collapsed on the floor. In a heap of petals.

(9)

In three weeks, Jude Marsini had acquired a mother. Two sisters. And had become a scribe to a Mormon priestess, who awakened his body at the age of forty in ways he hadn't thought possible. And most surprisingly of all: he had seemingly fallen in love with a woman who had been, until a few days ago, his friend's wife. Eman was different. Not because of how he felt towards her. But because of how she made him feel towards everything else.

Even with her face buried in his lap, Zina was not able to erase his awareness of his humanity. And the lack of the world's humanity. That constant streak of bleak consciousness that never left him.

Something about Eman could.

Something about Eman did.

MARKED

(1)

"My name is Osama. I'm the Chief Accountant of the ACA. I should have introduced myself earlier. Forgive me. It's been a busy few weeks."

Jude offered the man in the navy suit a seat.

"I'm afraid I can't stay. I just wanted to let you know that we appreciate having you as our dean, and that you can count on us for help whenever you need it."

*

In 2005, Rafiq al-Hariri, then Prime Minister of Lebanon, was killed in an explosion in Beirut along with twenty-one other people. It was Valentine's Day.

Shortly before his assassination, Syria's Foreign Minister visited Hariri and assured him that they were on his side and wanted to work closely with him. There is even a recording of this conversation.

Walid Jumblatt, veteran Lebanese politician, would later comment: 'When the Syrian regime intends to eliminate someone, they comfort them first.'

*

Jude decided he needed to act fast. He phoned

the Accreditation Commission and asked for an urgent meeting with Abdallat. A minute passed. The secretary confirmed he could meet at two o'clock.

At two, Jude walked into the Accreditation Commission and told the secretary that needed to print some photos.

"This is what we suspected. You are now cleared on our side, Dr. Marsini. But you need to understand, these people are very powerful and, sadly, they have many friends. In high and low places."

Jude nodded. Though he wasn't sure he fully followed exactly what Abdallat was saying.

"The moment they suspect you have betrayed them they will activate this network against you. My advice is simple: leave."

Jude felt his knees weaken. He had done this precisely so he would not have to leave. Where exactly would he go? Back to Syria? He had not avoided arrest in Jordan only to be imprisoned back home. And if not Syria, which part of the world would welcome him when all he had was a Syrian passport?

As Adel took him back to the university, Jude watched as the tarmac they drove over crumbled behind them. Falling away into a cavernous blackness. He kept his eyes forward. But all he could see was darkness before them too.

Adel's phone broke the deafening hum of tires and engine.

"Yes, sir."

"Yes, sir."

"Yes, Your Excellency."

Adel indicated left. He headed down a road leading in the opposite direction to the ACA. He mumbled something about having to run an errand before driving back to the college. Jude felt his heart beating faster. Adel was now dressed in military uniform. He shifted the gun in his holster. Jude's palms stuck to the leather seats.

He glanced at the lock on the passenger door. It was raised. Minutes. Hours. Days passed.

Adel stopped at a traffic light. It was red. Jude's signal to go.

He flung open the door. And ran.

(2)

He found himself in Swiefieh. Right across from Dubliners. An Irish bar popular with some of the ACA's students and foreign professors. Without thinking, he walked in and ordered a Heineken. Jude didn't drink. He had no moral position against it. It was just something his family didn't do. But at that moment, and in this place, his Damascene mores seemed light years away. He wondered what his next step should be. He couldn't go back home, that would be like walking into the eye of the storm. The thought that he may never see Ayşe or Şirin again made him feel like he was about to cry. The bartender brought him his beer. He took a long sip. He tasted broad beans.

None of this was helpful. He needed to be focused. Calculated. Careful. He needed someone to help him. Someone he could trust with all of this. Only one person came to mind.

*

He asked the taxi to wait for him as he walked into Rami's clinic. His first home in Amman.

"Jude, what are you doing here? You don't look well." In a summarised fashion, Jude shared with Rami everything that had transpired. His discovery. Abdallat's instructions. The car drive. His escape.

Rami understood. Jude had to leave. They would be coming for him.

"Who is 'they'? Aren't we just talking about people who are important in Lebanon?"

In a new suburb west of Amman, in an area called Dayr Ghbar, Rami had purchased a new house. He hadn't yet bought furniture, and the water was not yet connected. There was a fridge, but not much in it. He gave Jude the key. Rashid had been Jude's protector. But he would be loyal to the Lebanese. And to the money.

"Give me your phone, Jude."

Rami took out the battery. Removed the SIM card. And placed them both in the bin.

3

Dayr Ghbar was a well-organised suburb that stretched over the hills and valleys to the west of Amman. It took about twenty minutes for the taxi to arrive at the villa. It was dusty white. In the front garden stood an old olive tree. A tree that clearly belonged to an age when Dayr Ghbar had been part of the wilderness few Jordanians dared venture into. Inside, the villa was empty. It was also dusty white. This was perhaps where Rami planned to start his new life with a wife who could give him the children he craved.

Jude's thoughts were interrupted by the small sounds of a cat. In the back garden he found a kitten. Black. Thin. Hungry. Jude found a carton of milk in the fridge. It was still fresh. In the garden, he poured the milk into a small, curved piece of tile that seemed to have been surplus to the length of the roof. The kitten purred as she lapped. As Jude sat on the doorstep, he watched as numerous kittens entered the back garden, crawling out from under bushes, and through the fence. He poured more milk onto the broken tile.

*

Eman arrived at Rami's clinic not too long after Jude had left. She drove from there to Abdoun. When she rang the bell of the villa, a young girl opened the door. Her hair was black. Long. Tied up with a yellow ribbon. Her mother appeared behind her.

"I don't think his Syrian passport will help him now. His name is probably on the border anyway. But wait here."

Minutes passed. Eman stood in the corner of the dining room. Şirin was sitting at the table, watching the scene silently. Eman heard a baby crying. When Ayşe returned, she was carrying Jude's briefcase. She whispered something to Şirin, who stared up at her mother, and quietly left the room. When Şirin returned, she was carrying a small box.

Riyad Sabuni had died on the 23rd of December 2010. Ayşe had not registered his death anywhere. Not in Jordan. Not in Germany. He had been tall. Six feet. Fair complexion. Dark brown hair. He looked ten years younger in his passport picture than he did on the day he died.

Ayşe handed the box to Eman. It contained Riyad's German passport. Identity card. Money. And a small golden pendant.

"I don't want you to be in trouble in any way."

"I won't be. And for Jude's sake it would be worth it."

From Abdoun, Eman drove to the American Ambassador's residence. At the gate, a security officer asked why she was there. She told him she was there to see her friend, Zina. The guard spoke into his walkie-talkie and asked her to wait.

A woman emerged from the building. She was tall. Blonde. Athletic.

"I was about to leave. Come with me, we can speak in my car."

Eman told the woman she knew must be Zina about Dayr Ghbar. And the German passport. Zina looked concerned. She stared out of the window.

"Will you be leaving with him?"

"I wasn't planning to."

As a Syrian, no one would expect Jude to leave for Israel. The airport was too dangerous. Even if he was carrying a different passport. They may already have his picture. But, if he crossed the border in a diplomatic car, he may not even have to leave the vehicle. This was Zina's guess. But from Israel, where would he go?

There was silence.

Eman thought back to the last time she had seen

Jude. On the steps. How she had watched him watch her stretch out her feet. How much she had wanted to kiss him.

"His father has a place near Rome."

Using her phone, Zina searched for flights. Tel Aviv to Rome. There was one flight that evening. It stopped in Malta. Zina tapped on the glass partition. The driver turned on the engine. Eman opened the door and stepped out of the car.

"If you decide you want to join him, be in Dayr Ghbar at six."

*

Jude was still in the back garden playing with around seventy black kittens when he saw the car pull up through the fence. He recognised the white jeep.

The King Hussein Bridge, also known as the Allenby Bridge, stretches out over the Jordan River. It connects Jordan to the West Bank. The crossing officially closes at eight. On Saturdays it closes earlier. Zina had done her homework. It was a three-and-a-half-hour drive to Ben Gurion Airport. She had planned to drop him off, spend the night in Jerusalem, and return to Amman before Oliver returned from Cairo on Monday night.

Jude fell asleep moments after getting into the car. If he could not find respite in kittens, he would find respite in sleep. Zina was disappointed. But his willingness to sleep next to her she chose to see as a sign of trust. So, she cherished it.

4

Eman drove around Dayr Ghbar all afternoon. She only pulled into her driveway at seven o'clock. When she knew that Jude must have long departed. Something in her, so much in her, wanted to be there. To leave with him. To put her story in Amman aside. To start something new. But there were other voices. Stronger voices. Voices that valued her job. Her social status. Her dislike of irrational choices that would simply not let her leave.

This was all so familiar. She thought back to her decision to marry Rami. She had been conflicted. So, she had prayed. *Istikhara*. The prayer for seeking good. That night, she had dreamt she was walking in a field of salt. She kept wondering why there were no plants or trees. All she could see was salt. Her mother felt the dream was clear: she shouldn't marry Rami.

When she shared it with Rami, he laughed:

"Salt is a good sign, you can add salt to food, you can't add trees to anything. Be my salt."

Eman took a long shower. She put on her prayer clothes. She prayed. Istikhara. The prayer for seeking good.

That night, she dreamt she was in Jerusalem. At the

Dome of the Rock. She had always wanted to visit. She was wearing a white dress. On her right was Zina. She was wearing blue. On her left was Ayşe. She was in pine green. Sitting across from her was Jude. He was wearing a black suit. His tie was teal, a perfect combination of Zina's blue and Ayşe's green. Jude removed a ring from one of his fingers.

"Yes."

She said.

Though no question had been asked.

She was now on a beach. She was wearing nothing. She couldn't see the sea, but she could hear waves. Jude was lying next to her. His hand was between her legs. Caressing. Gently. He moved his body over her. She felt him inside her. She moaned. Softly. Loudly. The waves arrived. They seemed to be pulling him away from her, blending her pleasure with anxiety. She moaned. Softly. Loudly.

She awoke to the sounds of her own pleasure.

(5)

Jude Marsini slept all the way to Jerusalem.

Outside the car, the American flags and assurance from the consulate had guaranteed their diplomatic immunity. They had not been required to leave the car.

Inside the car, the glass barrier and dark tinted windows guaranteed their privacy.

Zina spoke to Jude as he slept. She had her head on his lap. Her hand within the folds of fabric at his waist. In between the words she was sharing, she drew him into her mouth. Slowly. Even spiritually. As though performing a ritual.

"How will you remember me? As a crazy, bored, ambassador's wife, who couldn't resist your taste? Do you have any idea what you taste like? Think of lemons, salty lemons, and cream. See, you can't blame me for wanting to taste you one more time. The more I taste you, the more I am open to the sky, the more it speaks to me, the more I can hear it."

She paused and then went back to caressing him.

"I'm just a woman who wanted to see God in her own way. I wanted to see God in my eyes, not

Joseph's eyes, not anyone else's eyes. Why is it so unacceptable for a woman to do this?"

She raised her head and saw he was still asleep.

"If you want to see God, you must be willing to see your desire. To become your desire. Without desire we are left to our fear. We become cowards. And cowards can't see God. They only see what they fear."

She placed him deep into her mouth. Then pulled him slowly out.

"You know, because of you, I am now a member of an exclusive club: Potiphar's wife desired Joseph. David desired Bathsheba. Let history record that Zina desired Jude."

She pressed him tightly. Jude's body suddenly jerked. His eyes opened wide. He looked down. The violet eyes looked back into his. On her cheek, rested a small white butterfly. *Pieris rapae*. He moved his hands to Zina's head and gently pushed her from him. She resisted for a few seconds, then pulled away.

"I'm going to miss you."

*

The plane to Rome was scheduled to depart at

eleven forty-five. They arrived at the airport a few minutes past ten. Zina handed him a black leather bag. It contained the box Eman had given her. And a few items she had added. A toothbrush. A comb. A travel size bottle of Old Spice.

"I almost forgot. I want you to have this."

She handed him a small brown stone. It looked like a dormouse.

(6)

In Abdoun, late that night, Ayşe and Şirin sat on a prayer carpet. They were both wearing white prayer clothes. The carpet was green and gold.

"Choose one."

"You choose, Mother."

"No, you should. Your heart is purer."

Şirin closed her eyes and chose a card. It was the Queen of Water.

"What does that mean, Mother? Is it a good sign?"

Ayşe was silent. A tear fell down her cheek.

They chanted.

La ilaha illa al-Nur.

There is no god other than The Light.

Over and over, until Şirin fell asleep. Curled on the carpet. Surrounded by petals.

Ayşe carried her to her bed. She placed her hand on her mouth. Recited a prayer. She moved her hand away from her face. And blew.

7

Eman's decision to travel to Italy was not based on the dream. It was because she had found Jude's briefcase in her car. She had forgotten to give it to Zina.

Inside, there was Jude's Syrian passport. Receipts. And a map of the location of Jude's house in Sperlonga. He must have printed it at the office.

Eman took this as a sign.

Without this, she would have had no clue where in Italy Jude was traveling to, and her dream, powerful as it may have been, had not been enough to convince her to get on a plane and follow him. But with a map in her hand, she could now purchase a ticket to Rome and meet him. There was a flight leaving in three hours.

She was getting into the taxi when her phone rang: Rami.

"Eman, do you know which flight to Rome Jude was supposed to take?"

"I'm not really sure. I think it was supposed to be the last plane out of Tel Aviv. It has a layover in Malta. Why are you asking?"

There was silence.

"Rami, what's wrong?"

(8)

Saint Paul left for Rome after three years of wandering in Arabia. His ship sank near the island of Malta. He and his fellow passengers survived and swam safely to the shore.

The year was 60 AD.

Jude Marsini left for Rome after three weeks of wandering in Amman. His plane crashed near the island of Malta. He and his fellow passengers died upon impact.

The year was 2011 AD.

Over the last one thousand, nine hundred, and fifty-one years, travel methods have significantly changed, but travel plans have not.

They are still irrelevant to our destination.

Movement Two

The Rage of Fatima

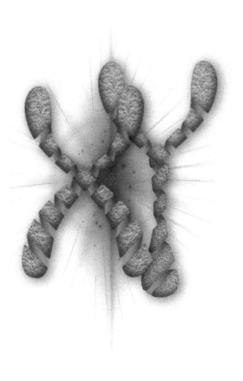

(1)

When I can't sleep, which is as frequent as my attempts to sleep, I retreat into my head. I come up with an intricate idea, the kind that has historic layers, erotic images, and subtle spiritual implications; the kind that says more about me than possibly anything else I do or say. Tonight, it occurs to me that there is, or was, a woman who became Playboy's Playmate in the very month I was born. And for reasons yet to be fully captured and explained, I conclude that there must be a connection between this woman and I. The idea is ticklish. I reach for my mobile to search for the Playmate of May 1980. Google does not hesitate. I am duly informed that the woman to whom I am existentially connected is Martha Thomsen. Not sure how, but Martha leads me to Tina Bockrath, Playmate of May 1990. Blonde with soft brown eyes, from Dayton, Ohio. She wants to visit Cairo, and I close my eyes and take her there. We have tea near the Pyramids. She's wearing a white, deep plunge jumpsuit, and sandals. I notice a golden anklet with a black lotus pendant as she pushes her feet deep into the morning sand. She smiles and asks if I realise that this is an invitation, and I wonder what it would be like to see her lying next to me instead of Lynx, my very black long-haired cat, who suddenly opens her eyes as though aware of my treacherous thoughts.

Though I'm now far sleepier, my spiritual sensibilities have awoken, reminding me of all the abusive men and tragic endings associated with the world of Playboy's models. I see sleazy hands, and sleazier offers. I feel tainted and unworthy. I recite a prayer, and I blow it in the direction of Martha, Tina, and all sister playmates, alive and dead.

Five hours later, I am ready to receive Sunday morning. I walk into the shower and reach for my organic plastic-free soap bars. You probably haven't heard about this, but there's a grand conspiracy to infuse human bodies with plastic, and I am one of the few living *Homo sapiens* to have discovered and aborted this plan. As millions buy milk, yoghurt, toothpaste, shampoo, and more in plastic containers that leach Bisphenol A, or BPA, into the contents they are meant to preserve, I use plastic-free alternatives for each of these products. BPA is fascinating and had it not been for the fact that it has carcinogenic properties, I would have encouraged any man who is willing to listen to me to consume food products in plastic containers. After all, BPA has been shown to cause men to become less masculine and even to reduce sperm count. And since I can't stand the vast majority of masculine qualities, mine included, and since I have also long felt that this planet is way too overcrowded, BPA would be the perfect prescription for both concerns.

My shower is always far too hot, and I walk out like

a wet red Martian. Unlike Kris Kristofferson, who searches on Sunday mornings for his 'cleanest dirty shirt', my wardrobe is full of pressed and colour-coded garments. I wear violet on Sunday because, obviously, violet is the first colour of the rainbow, and I pride myself for being in sync with the cosmos. It's 4:30 a.m. and I have ten minutes left before sunrise. I stand on my prayer carpet and perform the dawn prayer. It's composed of four movements, two voluntary and two mandatory. Each movement includes a combination of standing, kneeling and prostrating—each with distinct recitations. An ancestor of mine once wrote a treatise on the merits of lying down in between them, and out of genealogical fidelity, I lie down for a few seconds after completing the voluntary movements. I use specific verses for each prayer of the day, and I prefer verses in which God is referred to by the plural 'We' or the singular 'I'. I am, and always have been, an eccentric Muslim. Without eccentricity, my sense that I belong to the millions of Muslims I can't possibly identify with is enhanced, and my faith is eroded. Next, I reach for my mobile, and open a saved copy of the *Litanies of Days and Nights*, a collection of esoteric prayers that are said to have been compiled by various mystics and philosophers. Each litany invokes specific names of God, and angels that oversee each day of the week. There is even a specific planet, precious stone, and scent that are associated with each day.

Finally, it's time for breakfast. I am craving the

perfect combination of sweet and savoury, chilled watermelon with feta cheese, along with deep, black tea, sweetened with a touch of organic honey. I need about four cups before I am ready for the next part of my day, the early morning walk.

Southend is a small town located on the Thames Estuary in Essex. It's about forty miles from London, and it takes an hour by train to reach Fenchurch Street in southeast London. On most days, Southend is as boring as it is harmless, but on some days, it has a tranquil glow that settles deep inside your soul. My forty-minute walks begin near Priory Park and end at the entrance to the pier, allegedly the longest pier in the world, though I've never bothered to check the veracity of this frequently repeated claim. I walk briskly, and I usually think about what I plan on achieving, and avoiding, that day and on this first Sunday of June, my plan is simple: Try, yet again, to speak to my parents; write a blog on Syria's addiction to exporting Captagon to its neighbouring countries; and try, yet again, to finish reading *One Hundred Years of Solitude*. On the avoid list, the critical point remains COVID-19 which, in turn, entails avoiding human contact and washing my hands before, during, and after my departures from home. This virus is as mysteriously lethal as it is seemingly easy to avoid, and I am just as adamant at avoiding it now as I have been since late January when this sophisticated virus first arrived on the British Isles.

(2)

Of all the possible encounters that could carry with them bacteria and viruses, none was harder to avoid than Ana Rita Almeida Santos. Ana Rita is my Portuguese neighbour who, along with her husband, moved into Princess Court in December. Their flat is adjacent to mine, but because the building is U-shaped, the windows of their kitchen and living room sit right across from my large living room window. Tomas is a pilot, fat, short, bald, and smiling even when it makes no sense to smile. They are both in their early forties and do not appear to have any children, at least not here in Southend. A few days after moving in, I found a wallet dropped in the building's corridor, and it wasn't difficult to figure out that it belonged to Tomas. I knocked on his door, which was a big mistake, and handed him his wallet. A few minutes later, he arrived at my flat with Ana Rita, and spent hours talking to me about planes and flying in a comic version of Portuglish. "I am learning English since I was at..." Silence follows. He whispers *escola* several times and then his default smile becomes even brighter because he has clearly remembered the word he is looking for: "school, school!" I smile back, and Ana Rita ignores both of us. In fact, throughout the entire visit, she remained silent. I assumed she couldn't speak a word of English. Before leaving, Tomas held my hand tightly and, in essence, informed me that since he was never here and "couldn't do nothing about it", Ana Rita was my *irmã*. It was then, perhaps out of her desire to eliminate any possible misunderstanding, that Ana Rita finally spoke: "Sister, *irmã* means sister."

And so it was that at the age of forty, I acquired a sister who bore a striking resemblance to Karla Conway. At 4ft 11, Karla was Playboy's shortest playmate ever. And like Karla, my sister wasn't only short, she was also at least a 36D, though she dressed in a way that tried, unsuccessfully, to make this aspect of her figure less noticeable. I know I must sound vulgar, but you have to understand that this is a direct consequence of having been exposed, in fact over-exposed, to all things Portuguese over the past five months. First, it's the windows, did I already mention the windows? Ana Rita dresses very modestly outside of her home, but this should not be confused with how she dresses inside her home. For reasons that escape me, the way she dresses, or rather undresses, is directly correlated to Tomas being thirty-five thousand feet above sea level. When Tomas is in Southend, she lies on the couch in a plain T-shirt and jeans, and Tomas walks around in shorts, his hairy flesh appearing to move even when he isn't. When Tomas departs, however, Ana Rita lies on the couch wearing only her yellow panties. When Tomas is here, she cooks wearing a long black pleated dress. When Tomas departs, she prefers to cook only in an apron. Their large windows have no curtains and are only about fifteen meters away from my flat. It's an intrusion bordering on harassment. But I have made my peace with it, and five months later, I confess to being unsure as to what I would do if Tomas suddenly decided it was time to buy blinds.

My 'sister', mind you, does all this with an indifferent, nonchalant air. Not once have I caught her looking in my direction. It is as though my flat, my windows and I didn't exist. It gets more complicated because, again when Tomas is away, my bell rings and a plate, with an object wrapped in aluminium foil, is placed outside my door. At times, she is still there when I open the door, but she stands only long enough to smile, hand me the plate and walk away. This leads us back to the human contact I have trouble avoiding. Though I have tried repeatedly to explain to Ana Rita that in the age of corona she should not even approach my door, my objections are consistently ignored. At precisely two o'clock, after sensual scenes of her reading on the sofa, and fiddling about in the kitchen, a *prego no pão* arrives. And yes, I do ultimately open the door and carry the offering inside. And if my sin is ignoring the serious risks involved, my defence lies in the fresh bread roll full of thinly sliced steak, adorned with onions and beaming with the scent of garlic and pepper.

Prior to the prego, I would initially receive a *bifana* which I promptly inhaled until I found out it was loaded with garlic-seasoned strips of pork. I explained to Ana Rita that, as eccentric as I may be, no creative take on Islamic law would allow me to truly enjoy the bifana. She listened to me silently, as was typical of her, and the next day marked the birth of the prego. At times, especially on weekends, dessert is also delivered to my door. My favourite is *pudim de ovos*, a caramel custard with surprisingly strong flavours of lemon and cinnamon. I often have it instead of dinner, especially since it was only a few hours ago that I'd had a prego. I combine it with an extra-long espresso, long enough to last as I pretend to ignore the late evening scenes of Ana Rita reading and dozing off on the couch.

What is perhaps most peculiar about Ana Rita is the fact that she never seems interested in actually visiting me, or in me visiting her. Not that I would be willing to do so. I categorically would not. But the fact that over the last five months I have not once been invited to visit my neighbours, even when Tomas was in Southend, is a bit disconcerting. Perhaps it's a case of cultural misunderstanding. Perhaps in Portugal, finding a prego outside your door is in fact an invitation, a very genuine and sincere invitation. But since I won't bring it up, and Ana Rita is not too keen on having any form of conversation with me, the only living soul with whom I have any close encounters is Lynx, my Turkish Angora, who, like me, is exiled in the land of Southend.

(3)

My name is Idris Jamali, one of the millions of Syrians who left their homes after 2011 in search of a place where political disagreements are not treated as treason; and 'treason' isn't grounds for torture, sexual violence, and death. I left not because I was being targeted. I left because I could not suspend my awareness that Damascus, the city where my ancestors have lived since the fifteenth century, was now home to at least ten centres of state-sponsored violence against young women and men who, unlike me, were brave and idealistic. I knew these centres by name and location. I knew them because I was then, as I continue to be now, a freelance journalist with contacts amongst Syria's political elite, who were often too eager to share their stories with a person they regarded as both insignificant and harmless. They trusted me because they knew I was even more scared of what they had done than they were. And it appears that there really is something cathartic about the act of confession. In a sense, I was a priest in disguise performing the Sacrament of Penance, except that these sessions would end with heavy silence rather than with a prayer to absolve their sins. I knew exactly when I was at a restaurant or a coffee shop near these centres of death. I knew when I was driving down a road where one or more were located. I knew all this, and I could not stop my mind from visualizing the scenes that were taking place.

The scenes would arrive unexpectedly and were so overwhelming that I, at times, had to stop my car and try my best to not hyperventilate. God knows I tried to listen to my father's advice. He would repeat to me that the way I was thinking, the way I was seeing what was happening meant that I would either end up being arrested, or that I would have to leave the country. In either case, this would mean that I would never see my parents again. But how does one continue to write articles on the Syrian economy when the Syrian police were shooting at unarmed civilians? Even the foreign media outlets to which I sent regular pieces were now far more interested in news about the protests rather than the financial market. I was a trusted voice not only because I was very technical and detailed, but also because I could write in perfect English. My English was my mother's gift to our family; one of many gifts without which we would have been regular Damascenes, susceptible to various conspiracy theories and ultimately willing to accommodate any political leadership regardless of how ruthless and corrupt. It was because of my British mother that I could not see things like my father did. And it was because of how I saw things that I made the decision to leave before I found myself in one of the very centres that flooded my mind with such fear and disgust. My British passport, yet another gift from my mother, made it possible for me to travel first to Amman, and from Amman to London. London was far too polluted and expensive for any serious prolonged stay, so after a lengthy search for the closest reasonable alternative I found myself in Southend.

All of this seems like ancient history now. It's been more than eight years since I left Syria and settled, like Helen Mirren's grandfather, as an exile in Southend. My parents still live in Damascus. Both are in their seventies, and both are still far more dedicated to the serious rituals of life than I am or ever was. They cook, visit relatives, and my father still has a job; in fact, he has two. My Sunday phone calls are events I must mentally prepare for because my parents invariably succeed in making me feel guilty for having left them alone. As their only child, the least I was expected to do was to remain with them during their old age. I haven't even provided them with a grandchild who would do this on my behalf. Yes, I am not married, nor have I ever been. To understand this, you would have to know about my uncle, who was charming, charismatic and fiercely against the idea of marriage. But when he was in his mid-forties, a close friend of his died, and my aunts, sensing his moment of weakness, convinced him to go along with their arranged marriage plans. In less than six months after he was married, he looked like a bird, once wild and majestic, with now severely clipped wings. Not too long after, he had a stroke and by sixty he was gone. I watched what marriage had done to my uncle and I made the decision that I would never allow it to do this to me.

My weekly phone calls to my parents weren't only tense because of how guilty they made me feel, but also because the connection was always terrible, making any attempt to have a meaningful conversation with my mother, whose hearing was poor, even harder, and often entirely hopeless.

"Hello."

"Hello. Who is this?"

"Mum, it's me."

"What did you say?"

"It's me, Mum, it's Idris."

"Citrus?"

"Idris, Mum, it's Idris."

She shouts at my father. "Turn the TV down, I'm trying to talk on the phone."

"Mum, it's me."

"Idris, what a nice surprise. We were wondering if you would ever phone us again."

"Mum, I phone every Sunday."

"Subway?"

"Sunday, Mum, I phone every Sunday."

"Here, talk to your father. The connection is terrible."

"Idris, is everything okay? Are you washing your hands? Don't leave home without a mask. Do you need money?"

"Yes, yes, everything is okay. Don't worry about me, I'm very, very careful. Please just pray for me."

My mother is back on the phone, "What did you say?"

"Please pray for me, Mum. I said please pray for me."

"We pray for you every night."

Now tears are escaping my eyes. I pretend the connection has been cut off and I end the call. The tears are replaced with anger. Anger at the hideous Syrian regime and its thugs for separating me from my parents and reducing our communication to a barely audible conversation on WhatsApp.

I stare out of the window hoping to see something that will take my mind in a very different direction to Damascus and my parents. If only Ana Rita would appear, if only I could see her standing near her stove, like a Renoir painting of Suzanne Valadon, his petite and infamously wild muse. Instead, I see a young man. This is not even Tomas. Who on earth has dared to violate this building's isolation and walk into my Ana Rita's home? Something strange was going on, and I was as irked as I was curious to find out who exactly this man was.

(4)

As I continue to stare out of my window, Ana Rita suddenly appears. I instantly notice that she is uncharacteristically looking straight at me. I watch her approach and open her window, something she had never done before, and I stand frozen, like a rabbit caught in the headlights. Was she about to tell me off? Was she finally going to complain about all the times I had stared at her? She starts speaking, but I can't hear her. I nervously open my window and prepare for the worst.

"Dr. Idris, I am sorry to talk to you like this, but I need to share something with you, and I think this would be the safest way to talk."

Apart from a word or two, this was the first time I had heard her speak for any prolonged period. It was clear that she knew English far better than her husband, though she did have a distinct accent. I chose to ignore the erroneous title, thinking it was possibly a polite way of addressing neighbours in Portugal.

"Yes, of course. This is perfectly fine. I hope everything is okay?"

"Thank you, you are very kind. This is Miguel, my brother."

She says something to the young man standing not too far from her and he reluctantly waves at me. I smile and wave back.

"Miguel arrived today from Lisbon. I told him he now must stay here for two weeks. Because of the virus, you know? But he doesn't listen to me. Maybe he will, maybe he won't, I don't know."

"Yes, I heard about this. Everyone arriving now is required to do so."

I'm now starting to wonder how Miguel's arrival will impact my *pregos* and yellow garment scenes.

"Miguel shared a story with me. And I remembered that you are a doctor in Arabic."

"Not a doctor, but yes, I do know Arabic well."

"Dr. Idris, Tomas always says you are a very humble man. Well, I was hoping maybe you can help us with this book Miguel found. Someone told him it was in Arabic, and we don't know any Arabic."

She pronounced 'Arabic' with a misplaced stress on the second syllable, 'Araaabic'. It actually sounded quite sexy.

"Sure, I'm willing to help in any way I can. Why don't you take my phone number and this way you can send me pictures of the book, and I can send you back a translation."

I share my number with her as she punches the digits into her mobile. In a few minutes, my phone rings.

"Dr. Idris, I think it is better if I share the whole story my brother shared with me before I send you the pictures. Is that okay?"

"Yes, please go ahead."

It takes her about ten minutes to share a story that seems to have come straight out of a Portuguese thriller. Her brother, who is 'not educated like her'– that's her description–works on a construction site. He was hired last year to work on the restoration of an ancient site known as the Castle of Ourém–she had to spell it because I couldn't come up with a spelling that matched how she pronounced it. As Miguel was repairing the walls of one of the chambers, a prison in fact, he found a metal object that seemed as though it had been deliberately shoved and hidden in between the stones. The object looked like 'a silver cucumber'–she must have meant a cylinder–and inside it there was 'a roll of leather', which sounded like a parchment scroll. He took a few quick pictures of the scroll, but then had to shove the object back into the wall because his supervisor arrived and called him to a meeting. At the meeting, the workers were informed that they had to suspend the project and leave because the authorities had closed the site due to the coronavirus outbreak. He showed the pictures he took to a friend, who is 'educated, and a dentist', and the dentist informed him that it looked like Arabic. When he turned up in England at his sister's flat, unemployed and now out of money, he shared the story with her. It was then Ana Rita remembered that her neighbour wrote articles on Syria, and therefore must speak Arabic, and so must be able to figure out what this 'book' her brother found was, and—and this is the crux of the matter as far as her brother was concerned—whether or not it had any monetary value.

Next, three images arrive on my WhatsApp. The first is of his hand holding a silver cylinder which is about four to five inches in length and one and a half inches in diameter. The second is of the rolled-up scroll, which appears yellowish and browning at the edges. And the third is of a small segment of the open scroll with the camera very close to the object so as to produce an image of only part of a line. It is Arabic, and the script reminds me of the Birmingham Quran manuscript. I do a quick search for the Birmingham Quran, and my hunch is confirmed. They were both written in Hijazi script, one of the earliest Arabic scripts that was used in the seventh century, during the time of Prophet Muhammad. The script has no dots, and it consistently slopes to the right. The ink is brown. Two words are visible: ''an', meaning 'on the authority of', and 'al-Zahra', a female adjective meaning 'the Blossoming One'.

I'm not quite sure what I should share with Ana Rita. My journalistic instinct is to find out more about the exact location where her brother found the cylinder, even as I convince his sister that this has no possible value and that it was probably placed there by a playful tourist. I phone back and share my conclusions, and she sounds both relieved and disappointed. She clearly didn't want her brother to see this as a possible source of income which would encourage him to do something illegal, like perhaps trying to steal the cylinder and sell it, but at the same time the passing promise of unexpected wealth had obviously played with her imagination.

With Ana Rita and Miguel no longer focused on the scroll, I am now free to become obsessed with it. I have long wanted to make my name as a very different type of journalist. Documenting the discovery of an ancient manuscript may well be exactly the kind of topic that will propel me out of the dark world of covering Syria's economy and politics.

I spend the next few hours, which were supposed to be spent on Syria's Captagon industry, researching the Castle of Ourém and Arabic manuscripts in Spain and Portugal. By six, I'm exhausted and hungry. I conclude that I need help. For one thing, I can't speak Portuguese or Spanish. Google delivers. I find a woman—Iranian judging by her name—who specialises in Andalusian literature at Oxford. Her departmental profile and research seem to be completely relevant to what I'm looking for, though I'm not entirely sure exactly what that is. I find her email address and send her a message. To lure her into answering me, I decide to attach the images shared by Miguel, though I emphasise that I am sharing all of this in complete confidence.

Next, and in the absence of an exquisite *prego*, I must make something to eat. In a deep iron pan, I pour lots of olive oil, then add organic chickpeas from a carton package. I wait a few minutes, then add cherry tomatoes, diced garlic, and a sprinkle of chili pepper. I stir it all with a wooden spoon and throw a few pita breads in the oven. I'm too hungry to squeeze lemons to add to cold water—my favourite drink—so I just sit at the table and inhale this nameless dish I learnt from a Lebanese friend ages ago.

Later, I make black tea, and I sit on my couch and watch several episodes of Frasier, the only possible replacement for watching Ana Rita move around her flat. I fall asleep with the TV still on. At about midnight I wake up, perform the night prayer, and climb into bed. Lynx follows and makes herself comfortable not too far from my pillow. Tonight, I fall asleep quickly, and I dream of castles.

(5)

Today, I am travelling to Oxford. An email I found in my inbox from Dr. Fatima Tabrizi informed me that she was indeed interested in what I had shared, and that she was ready to meet me on Monday for lunch. I replied saying I could be in Oxford by noon, and in minutes she had confirmed. And so, my journey to the land of Waugh's *Brideshead Revisited*, where Charles Ryder once met Sebastian Flyte, begins. I take the C2C to Fenchurch, the underground from Tower Hill to Paddington and by eleven, I am on a Virgin train to Oxford. Fatima wants to meet me at Mansfield College, which I will never be able to find on my own. So, I take a taxi from the station, and it drops me off near the front gate.

The gate is closed. I inform a porter, who is wearing a mask and comes out to meet me, who I want to see, and he asks me to sanitise my hands and wait. A few minutes later, a woman wearing a white scarf, and a long grey blazer dress appears. The porter hands her a notebook, and she scribbles something on it and signs her name. He opens the gate, and she smiles warmly. Nothing is more noticeable about her features than her sea-green eyes. I don't usually notice eyes, but these particular eyes take over everything. They remind me of a famous National Geographic picture of an Afghan girl with a striking gaze. Fatima appears oblivious to social distancing and other precautions. She leads me towards one of the sandstone buildings, up two flights of stone steps to the 'Tower Room'. The door opens onto an elegant lounge with cream armchairs, a fireplace, and large windows overlooking the grounds. She gestures to me to sit down. She walks to the coffee machine and comes back with two espressos. I like that she didn't ask me if I wanted some. She places the cups on a coffee table and sits near me. Something in me wants to find another seat at least two meters away, but I restrain myself, and focus on her eyes.

"So, here you are. The man who kept me up all night. I'm going to ask you a few questions which I hope you will answer as clearly as possible."

Her directness alarms me. I feel like nothing I had learnt in Damascus, the city of elusiveness, will help me here. She doesn't wait for me to answer or express my agreement.

"Are you in possession of this manuscript?"

"No."

"Where is the manuscript?"

"In a wall in Castle Ourém."

"So, the man who found it left it there?"

"Yes, officials appeared, and he shoved the cylinder back in the wall, right where he found it."

"How unfortunate."

"It is indeed."

"Who else knows about this?"

"Let's see. The man who found it, a dentist, his sister, me, and now you. So altogether, five people."

Fatima, who only a few minutes ago had appeared as though she was ready to invite me to lunch *and* dinner, was now standing and obviously asking me politely to leave. She had expected me, I now realised, to arrive with the manuscript, and she had planned to lure me into entrusting it to her. But now I was suddenly of no value.

"We should stay in touch by email. Please don't hesitate to send me a message if anything comes up."

"I will."

I walk towards the door, and I press the silver button to release the lock. I look back, hoping to get one final glimpse of her eyes, but she was now standing near the window and staring outside, entirely oblivious to my departure.

(6)

Some fifteen minutes from my home is Southend Airport. There was a time when it would have been fairly easy to fly out from Southend to Portugal, but since mid-March very few planes depart and land at this airport. For reasons that are entirely unclear to me, you can now only travel to Bucharest and Vilnius from Southend. Unstoppable Heathrow, on the other hand, has a flight that departs every Tuesday at 3:10 pm, and arrives in Lisbon at 5:55 pm. To reach Heathrow from Southend, you must travel to Fenchurch and then you can either take the underground from Tower Hill all the way to Heathrow using the Piccadilly line from Paddington, or you get off at Paddington and take the Heathrow Express all the way to Terminal 1, which is of course what I choose to do. As my father would say, if you must travel, travel in style.

By now, you should have realised that I am a very impulsive person, and since I am neither a husband, nor a father, nor even an employee in the traditional sense, I can get on a plane and leave without having to inform anyone. There are only two exceptions to this Bohemian freedom; the first comes in the form of a cat, and the second in the form of a fear. I explain to Ana Rita on the phone that I need to travel because of an article I am writing, which on some level is not completely a lie, and since I am a 'doctor in Arabic' as she likes to see me, I am expected to travel whenever my job requires. She graciously agrees to pass by my flat twice a day and feed Lynx. I leave my keys under the mat of her door with a thank you card. Lynx, I know, will hate all of this, and will probably stop sleeping next to me for a few days as punishment, but it's still better for her to be irked and fed, than to remain alone in her kingdom, but sleep hungry.

The second obstacle to impulsive travel is a fear which involves an overall hatred of heights and of the idea of being in a vehicle that could, in theory, fall out of the sky at any minute and for countless reasons. My fear requires a very special 'travel litany' which I make sure I read seven times before I leave my home. I must also write a special prayer on the door of my apartment. I count how many payers I have so far scribbled, and I find that this will be the ninth time I have left Southend over the last eight years. I say goodbye to Lynx and walk out.

You might be curious as to how and why I decided to travel to Lisbon today. It wasn't actually a difficult decision to make at all. On the way back from Oxford, with the words of Fatima replaying in my head, I reached for my phone and booked a flight there and then. Not too far from Lisbon, there is a priceless manuscript waiting for someone to discover it, or more accurately to rediscover it. I plan on being that person. The manuscript will place me, as I rightly deserve, in the annals of great discoveries, and free me once and for all from my exile in the land of Southend. The fame and fortune this will bring me will allow me to buy a studio in Vienna and have Viennese coffee at Café Landtmann. No, I haven't actually had breakfast at the Landtmann, but if you read Ibbotson's *The Morning Gift*, or Michener's *Poland*, you will know exactly what I'm after. This is a place rich in history which prides itself on the slogan: *The only egg we do not serve is the one from Columbus.* I confess that the fact that it was Freud's favourite café does make it a bit less attractive. This, however, is completely offset by its *Maroniblüte*, a waffle loaded with sour cherries and chestnut mousse which is, in essence, the equivalent of paradise for all sincere lovers of chestnuts. Nearly a quarter of a century ago, when I was still a child in Damascus, my aunt would place chestnuts on the *soba*, a Turkish traditional oil-burning stove, and I would wait until they made a popping sound, then pick one up, peel it quickly, and take a deep bite of the still hot chestnut. Ripe ones would melt in your mouth and send you straight to chestnut bliss.

Don't misunderstand, however, this is not purely motivated by base human instincts. There is clearly a historic, and possibly even a religious value to this manuscript which cannot be ignored. A story waiting for a detective journalist like me to unravel and explain. My mind is tantalised by all of these possibilities, as a speaker on the train announces that we have arrived at Terminal 1.

Airports remind me of what I visualise life after death to look like. I imagine that the moment we die, we find ourselves at a place very similar to an airport. Each of us has a specific flight we must board. Some will travel economy, and a few will travel first class. Some of us push a cart loaded with large bags, and others carry only hand luggage. Everyone has a serious, sombre look and is focused on their ultimate destination. I, too, was in an intensely focused state as I checked in and went through security. I expected to see far fewer travellers, but with the exception of the masks, which almost everyone else had on, this could easily have been a day in the pre-COVID-19 age. I finally reach the departure gate. There are around twelve other passengers waiting to board, and all are sitting a few meters away from each other. I settle in the chair and decide I should read the travel litany again.

You are the companion of the journey. In Your Name does this plane take off, and in Your Name does this plane land.

Suddenly, my recitation is interrupted when I realise someone has decided to violate all guidelines to the contrary and sit right next to me.

"It looks like you are traveling to Lisbon, too. How interesting."

I stare at the sea-green eyes and I, the Damascene

who is never at a loss for words, find myself experiencing a rare moment of complete speechlessness.

(7)

Onboard, I am seated on a row of my own, and I'm glad to see that Fatima has been seated at least twelve rows in front of me. Plane rides unleash a collection of constantly evolving stories and references in my mind. Today, my flight to Lisbon begins with recollections of a pilot who decided that life had not been worth living after his mistress broke off with him. Naturally, the ideal way to respond was to depart this world and take with him at least two hundred passengers. Locks that are designed to prevent suicidal passengers from entering the cockpit work in favour of pilots with suicidal tendencies. In this particular story, the pilot diligently waited until his co-pilot departed to the toilet, an inevitable event, then locked the door and proceeded to enact a carefully rehearsed crash in the Indian Ocean. Mind you, it was a very considerate plan, and he went out of his way to ensure that passengers would not actually witness the horrific crash. He first flew above forty thousand feet, forty-five to be exact, until, twenty-three minutes later, the oxygen ran out and all crew and passengers experienced a fine state of hypoxia. With everyone now either dead or unconscious, he proceeded to descend to a very low altitude to avoid radars and, more importantly, to not disturb the sleep of his country's officials with the disruptive news of a plane flying way off its scheduled course. Six hours later, the plane finally disappeared into an ocean with valleys that dip as low as four thousand feet. Equally dramatic, yet far less sensitive, was another recent pilot's suicide into the French Alps. At least in this case, he made sure everyone knew he was far too depressed to be flying a plane. But is it really reasonable to expect airlines to constantly check the mental wellness of their pilots? After all, it's enough that they have to constantly check and maintain their planes which, and I apologise for sharing too much information, are really not very trustworthy machines.

These stories conflate and inflate as I start recalling other stories of random, mostly unexplainable mechanical failures that bring planes down even as their passengers dream about the holidays they carefully planned, and the loved ones they are eager to meet. Planes as majestic as the Concorde can crash in less than two minutes from something as trivial and unexpected as debris on the runway. I kid you not. Even ice crystals, one of nature's most visually intriguing phenomena flaunting hexagonal columns, hexagonal plates, dendritic crystals, and diamond dust, can turn deadly and cause a sudden stall, bringing down a state-of-the-art aircraft into the Atlantic Ocean. The problem is I read far too much, to the extent that I am aware of exactly what happens when tons of metal, kerosene and human bodies smash into the sea. Even your seatbelts, which you are constantly reminded to keep on, can slice you in half.

I drown in these unpleasant stories on this Tuesday afternoon as I avoid looking out of my cabin window, not only because they are replaying in my head, but also because I would like history to note that despite everything I knew about these dangerous and unreliable vehicles, I still chose to travel by plane for the selfless cause of historical discovery. Priceless manuscripts do not belong in ancient walls. They belong with researchers and truth-seekers. Eventually, they may even belong in the professional hands of renowned auctioneers. The thought of an auction at Sotheby's, and the price this ancient manuscript would sell for is enough to keep me distracted until the plane safely lands at Portela Airport.

As we disembark, I notice Fatima walking ahead of me. I deliberately didn't think about her during the trip. The thought of a co-explorer isn't pleasant at all, but my Damascene instincts are now telling me that I had to make the best of this and 'have lunch with her before she has dinner with me', a Damascene saying which, in essence, means in this context that I need to outsmart any attempt by her to exclude me and claim this discovery to be her own.

After clearing immigration and customs, there was another line that ended at a desk where four officials wearing masks were sitting.

"Have you encountered any sick people?"

"No."

"Do you feel sick?"

"No."

"Fever?"

"No."

"Coughs?"

"No."

A thermometer is raised to my head, and my temperature is taken with just a click. I apparently do not constitute any health risk, and the official gestures to me to leave. My next stop is at Avis, where I am supposed to pick up my Fiat 500. A figure in a headscarf is already there before me. This is becoming very uncomfortable, but I will stay calm and civil. She can hire as many cars as she wants. In the end, she can't possibly find the manuscript without me.

My Fiat is silver with a manual stick. Since I never drive in the UK, for obvious reasons involving the British insistence on driving on the wrong side, I look forward to setting off. It's a beautiful day, and I roll down the window and tune in to a radio station that is playing Portuguese *fado*, expressive, melancholic, and reminiscent of Abd al-Halim, my favourite Egyptian singer. Every now and then, another Fiat, white and convertible, passes me by. Its top is down, and a woman wearing shades and a scarf that is dancing with the wind, smiles, but I ignore her, and focus on the road. My destination is Pousada Ourém, a three-star hotel which is an hour and a half from Lisbon and a three-minute walk from Castle Ourém. It has terrible reviews, but it's the closest I could find to the castle, and besides, I don't trust reviews because I can't see myself writing one. I made reservations for three nights, but I might end up staying only one. It all depends really on how easy or difficult it's going to be to enter the castle and find the wall Miguel described.

At about eight thirty in the evening, two Fiats park, almost simultaneously, at the Pousada Ourém. I walk in carrying my bag without bothering to leave the door open for the woman walking behind me. I am usually a gentleman in the most sophisticated sense, but I'm far too anxious to think about manners.

"Good evening. Are you together?"

Fatima answers before me, "Good God, of course not."

I had been feeling harassed; now I'm also feeling insulted.

We are each handed a key with a large metal ball attached to its ring. This place is clearly still operating in a pre-card age. I head to my room, drop my bag, and wash my face. I decide I will pray sunset and night prayer together before I sleep, and I head straight out. I find Fatima wearing jeans and carrying a leather bag slung over her shoulder. She looks back at me and smiles.

"It looks like you can't wait until the morning either."

"It looks like you are adamant at following me everywhere I go."

"I haven't followed anyone since I was three. We just happen to have the same destinations."

"Yes, it's all coincidental, isn't it?"

"I propose we put aside our wit and sarcasm, and in the interests of a productive evening, start working together as a team."

It irks me that she now sounds more Damascene than I do, but her offer is sensible, and I nod my head in agreement. A warm dusk breeze reminds me that I am no longer in Southend, and we walk in silence on the winding stone road leading to the castle above.

8

Five minutes later, we reach a large triangular structure, standing between two towers flanking the entrance to our right, and an older looking tower on a hill to our left.

"This is the palace of Count Afonso of Ourém. It's fifteenth century and it's not what we are looking for."

I nod, as though I am very aware of this fact. I actually did do a lot of research, but more on the history of the place than its architecture. The truth is I'm surprised by how vast it all seems now. What I should have done was find out more about where exactly Miguel was working when he found the cylinder. The prison Ana Rita mentioned could be anywhere. My excuse is I didn't want to seem too interested, and risk fanning Miguel's curiosity.

Fatima climbs the steps in the direction of the larger tower, and I follow. She seems very fit and determined. The tower has a dark wooden door, and Fatima walks straight to it.

"If we can't go in from this door, there should be another door further down."

She takes out a torch from her bag, and hands it to me.

"Switch it on and point it at the door, please."

She first tries to push the door, but it's clearly locked. She then removes a butter knife from her bag—my guess is this belongs to the hotel down the hill since she couldn't have been carrying it on the plane. She shoves it inside the large keyhole, moves it in various directions, then tries pushing again.

"This is called breaking and entering."

She points the knife at the torch I am holding and smiles.

"And that is called accessory to a crime. Let's try the other door."

The door we just examined was under one of the castle towers, and we head now to the two towers on the other side. The full moon was only four nights ago, so there's enough moonlight to see our way around. Fatima walks fast as though she has the whole site memorised. The door we stop at is part of the connecting wall rather than under a tower like the previous one was. She pushes, and it opens straight away. She turns to me with a beaming smile, like a child who just found a toy she was looking for. The courtyard inside is fairly large and triangular in shape. It's empty, except for a small square stone structure, and steps near it leading to a space underground. Against the wall connecting the two towers is metal scaffolding, and evidence of a fairly intensive restoration project that was abruptly stopped.

"This square bit is the fountain, and the steps must go down to the large underground cistern."

I nod again, but something in me is starting to think that it was going to be fairly impossible to find what we are looking for. The place is too big, and the possibilities of where the cylinder may be are endless. But we have to start somewhere.

"The underground cistern is probably where the prison once was."

"It's a cistern… a place where water is stored."

"Maybe they drowned people underneath or tortured them. What if it's not always full of water?"

Before she can object, I head across the patchy grass courtyard toward the stone steps leading underground. The smell of damp rock and mildew hits me immediately. Images of torture chambers in Syria flood the darkness, descriptions I'd heard of women being led into basements fill all the spaces the torch doesn't touch. I hear Fatima calling me, but in a sudden, almost trance-like state, I continue to descend. I reach what seems to be a chamber, with a grate in the ceiling through which I can see the moonlight. The floor is slippery with a thin sheen of stagnant water. I scan the walls of what has now become, in my mind, a Damascene dungeon. The quiet is more terrifying than any noises I can imagine. A sudden shower of stones behind me startles me from my stupor. I look up at the grate, which is now blocked by a figure.

"You can't be serious, Idris."

It's Fatima. My heart resumes its beating.

"I told you, it's not down there. No manuscript would survive the humidity below. The place we are looking for is in one of the towers. And I'm pretty certain I know which one. Can you come back up and help me figure out where north is? There's a fountain up here, if you fancy a swim while you're at it."

Mortified at my own stupidity, I climb back up into the open air, and taking deep, but I hope also inconspicuous breaths, I look above at the clear night sky, eager to make amends for my foolishness. In seconds, I find Polaris.

"North is in the direction of both these towers. The one behind us would be the southern tower. The northwest tower is the one to our left with the Portuguese flag flying over it."

I feel redeemed. My obsession with astronomy was

not in vain.

"Perfect, this then is the tower of Doña Mencía."

"Who?"

"Doña Mencía, the Spanish wife of a Portuguese king. She was actually imprisoned in this tower."

She walks inside the tower, and climbs up the ancient steps, and I follow as I point the torch in her direction. "Please be careful," I repeat more than once, though in my mind, it seems more likely that I would trip or miss a step. We reach a rectangular space with a ladder leaning against one of the walls. On the ground, there's a toolbox, and a few empty plastic water bottles.

"This must be where Miguel was working when he was called out by his supervisor. Maybe he was standing on the ladder when he spotted the cylinder…"

"Possible, though it seems too easy… Look, I don't do well with ladders. Can you climb up and see if anything looks promising?"

Though not a fan of heights myself, I finally feel like she appreciates my presence, and I climb up the ladder's steps, eager to be the one who locates the cylinder first.

"Not so fast please," she says to me as she holds the ladder steady with both hands. I use the torch to carefully examine the walls. I start with the one in front of me, then move my hand, right, back and left. Fatima's eyes are following the light. We pause, more than once, when we hear noises outside, but they all prove to be either imagined or innocent. No one is onto us. We resume our scanning of each wall. Nothing seems different or unusual. Just an endless stream of stones. I start again, focusing once more on the wall right in front of me. Suddenly, Fatima cries out.

"Wait! Go back. That looked like a shape."

I move my hand back a few inches, and the light falls on a faded image of a hand stencilled on the stones. It's rusty brown, and difficult to see even with the torch pointed straight at it.

"Look for something between the stones around it."

I notice a small round cavity. I point the torch at it, and the light hits a metal object. I feel my heart beating faster. Neither of us say anything, though it's clear to us both that we have found what we are looking for. Holding the torch between my teeth, I carefully insert my finger inside and pull the object out. It resists for a few seconds, then it comes out along with gravel and dust. I climb down the ladder, and hand it to Fatima. She blows off some of the dust,

262

and then places it in a small plastic bag.

"Aren't you going to open it?"

"Later, at the hotel. I think we should leave now."

We walk out of the castle, and in minutes we are back on the road leading down to the hotel. We are both silent, though my mind is buzzing with numerous thoughts. These are disturbed by the headlights of a car driving up the road toward us. My chest tightens. Surely, just locals out for a night-time drive. But as it approaches, the lights flash blue. It would probably take three reincarnations of life outside of the Middle East to erase the type of anxiety and fear that kick in when a Syrian man is confronted by a police car pulling up in front of him. These may well be the last seconds of life as he knows it. Everything that might follow this could easily be set back in that underground dungeon.

Two men in police uniform rush out of the car, and repeat words in Portuguese. "I think they want us to get in the car," I whisper. Fatima doesn't answer, but she seems surprisingly calm and composed as she follows their instructions. She clearly grew up in a democracy, I think as the policeman slams the car door behind me.

The police station at Ourém is located in a characterless white building. We were both asked to sit next to a large table. And for over an hour, the place is full of masked men in uniform who seem to regard us with contempt or indifference. Clearly no one here perceives us as constituting a threat of any kind. No one even bothered to search us.

A man wearing a suit finally shows up. He's not wearing a mask. Maybe he's too important to be wearing one, maybe he just couldn't find one that would fit over his enormous, jet black moustache. He lifts Fatima's handbag, and then empties its contents on the table. He raises the knife and examines it carefully, then he looks at both of us as if saying in silence, "I know exactly what you planned on using this for." He then reaches to the plastic bag and tips out the cylinder.

Suddenly, the phone rings. The mask-less man walks away from us and answers. He repeats *"Sim"* often, and then hangs up. He approaches us again and places the objects on the table back in Fatima's bag.

"Eles estão vindo para você."

Without looking at me, Fatima whispers, "He is saying they are coming to get us."

Ten minutes later, we are escorted to a white van. This ride is longer and along the way, white road signs inform us that we are heading in the direction of the town of Fátima.

Less than an hour later, and after our temperatures had been taken again at the gate of a large complex of white buildings flanking a tall steeple lit by floodlights, we are sat in a large room with deep buttoned leather sofas, wine-coloured, like the heavy curtains hung across the enormous Venetian windows. A young man in black robes shows up with two cups of tea. I figure that if it contains some type of poison, it's at least a prestigious way to die. We are both too tired to wonder too much about why we are here. We know we will soon find out.

A tall figure wearing a black cassock with scarlet piping and a scarlet sash shows up. I've watched enough movies to recognise that he is a cardinal. This particular clergyman had short silver hair, nostrils that were far too big for his face, and eyebrows reminiscent of Stalin's moustache. A nun walks to his right, careful to remain a few steps behind him. They approach us and greet us with their hands moving to their chest. We stand up and repeat the gesture. They are followed by two men carrying handheld receivers who deliberately avoid any eye contact with anyone. It's a scene out of a Tarantino movie, and it's lacking only in the fact that no one has yet been killed.

The cardinal speaks slowly and pauses between sentences long enough for the nun, with her pear-shaped body, and sparrow-like features, to interpret. Fatima keeps her knowledge of Portuguese to herself and listens attentively.

"His Eminence Cardinal Saraiva welcomes you to the Sanctuary of Fátima, but would like to know why a professor from Oxford and a journalist were looking for an object at Castle Ourém."

This cardinal is clearly well informed. He continues to speak, and she continues to interpret.

"His Eminence would like to know who informed you that there was an object at the castle."

More Portuguese.

"His Eminence would like to know what is inside the cylinder you found at the castle."

And more.

"His Eminence would be very appreciative to both of you if you could inform him of the sequence of events that led you to carry out this very bold act, bold and illegal act, at Castle Ourém."

The nun stops just before I make the decision that if she repeats one more "His Eminence" I will walk out of the room.

Fatima, realizing that I have no intention of answering any of the cardinal's questions, sits upright and proceeds to speak in a professorial Oxfordian accent.

"Please inform His Eminence that we appreciate his kindness and hospitality, and that I will share with him the entire story that explains tonight's events. I only ask in return for his willingness to consider what I will propose at the end."

The cardinal, like me, is clearly impressed with Fatima's voice. Oxfordian English leaves an impression on you even if your knowledge of English is non-existent. The nun interprets, and he moves his head in agreement signalling that he would be willing to consider her offer. The nun faithfully proceeds to interpret his head movements.

"His Eminence is willing to consider your offer."

The young man returns, this time with a large tray. He places two deep dishes in front of us as the nun proudly explains:

"*Chanfana de Borrego*. A lamb stew made by the best cook in Fátima, Father Guilherme."

She pauses, as though to recollect the exact English words she intends to use.

"The food is blessed twice. First because it was made by Father Guilherme, and second because it was made in the Sanctuary of Fátima."

We smile in gratitude. Fatima asks to use the restroom, and one of the men with the walkie-talkies guides her to a door at the far end of the room. The cardinal folds his arms and leans against his chair; the nun opens a small English-Portuguese dictionary as though eager to review her own interpreting performance; and I ignore both of them and proceed to devour my double-blessed *chanfana*.

(9)

Like almost everything else in my life, I can think of two ways to answer the cardinal's intrusive questions. The first is raw—reminiscent of me returning to Mansfield from an early morning run. My shoes still carrying the scent of grass, my breasts eager to be set free from the dreadful compression of an expensive hideous sports bra, my skin wet with strong Persian sweat, and my ears muffled beneath the fabric of my headscarf. I take everything off, even my Apple watch, even my cotton knickers, and I collapse naked on my bed. The blinds are shut, but the morning breeze opens them just enough to seduce the wandering eyes of young posh blonde English boys. The idea is sweet, and it slides down, along with my sweat, below my navel. The survivalist lecturer inside my head reminds me that in the age of camera phones, it would be wiser for me to get dressed, but my hand now has taken over, and it's too late for common sense to intervene.

Besides, who the fuck cares what I privately visualise in my head? I am just as hopelessly moulded by Western standards of dos and don'ts as you are. In fact, I am, sadly, one of those boring Western pseudo-humans who will live and die without having even seriously contemplated breaking a single law. So, if you wish to judge me, I judge you back as a recycled hypocrite. No one is asking you to agree with me. You can stick to Masters and Johnson and their stale sex research. I would rather, at least on this particular note, stick with the Quran which promises me, when I finally leave this synthetic planet, gorgeous youths, still radiating the beauty of their mothers, and as irresistible as 'scattered pearls'.

These were my random thoughts as I returned from a quick trip to the bathroom. As you might have guessed, I decided that Cardinal Saraiva and his penguin would rather listen to my polished, historically accurate, experientially false account. To hear about why I am truly here, and why it is important for me to locate an ancient Arabic manuscript that appears to have a woman quoted in it, would be to invariably conclude that I am a leader of a special Muslim branch of Pussy Riot, some sort of feminist punk protestor giving the finger on YouTube to the latest religious equivalent of Vladimir Putin. Truth be told, I have often admired their leader Maria Alyokhina, a poet who doesn't give a shit about protecting a position at Oxford as I sadly do. In fact, I would gladly replace any of my posh young English boys who come to life in my head after my early morning runs with this rebellious Russian beauty.

You see, the answer to the cardinal's question of why I am here would involve an exposé on the relentless mutilation of what I'd called my religion from without and within, and the shot at redemption the scroll appears to present. Like Maria, I am far beyond sickened at how men in positions of authority—and I emphasise men—have fucked over all things sacred in the name of whatever gives them the most power, and how the God I once passionately believed in seems to allow all this to take place. But I'm not sharing any of this with a priest.

And so, I relate the polished version. Polished—reminiscent of me in my classroom, wearing a white headscarf, and repeating 'well done' to my undeserving privileged students.

"Your Eminence, my colleague and I are here because we heard, quite by accident, about the presence of a cylinder in one of the walls of Castle Ourém. A man who was part of a construction team at the castle found it and then informed a relative of his who happened to be my colleague's neighbour. He, in turn, reached out to me, and we both independently decided to try to personally locate this cylinder. We met at the castle this evening, and after searching in various places, we were fortunate enough to find it. Hours later, we were transported to this room. The reason I was intrigued enough to do this is because from the few images the construction worker had taken of the scroll inside this cylinder, I could tell it was potentially a very important ancient Arabic manuscript."

I pause and watch them soak in my words. The nun slowly interprets and appears as suspicious as she is careful.

"I realise, we both realise, that we should have done this differently, but at times the proper method entails unleashing a swarm of intransigent bureaucrats who are unable to see the wider implications of what is at stake. I have no doubt that in your long illustrious career, your Eminence, you have often had to deal with such figures. People who were unable to see the grand objectives you were after. Had I had direct access to your Eminence, I would certainly have communicated with you first."

Yes, I am now massaging his ego. Nothing is more reliable in men than their love to be seen as lions, even when they barely qualify as bushbabies. I pause for a few seconds and assess the impact of my words on him. I confess I wasn't sure if the nun's interpretation would transmit everything I was trying to convey. But he's right where I want him—in the mood for a gracious gesture.

"The long answer to your questions, your Eminence, would involve, I am afraid, a lengthy presentation on the significance of Castle Ourém, the town of Fátima, Portugal on the eve of the reconquest, and how all of this may or may not be linked to the contents of this cylinder. This leads me to my offer which I hope you will be kind enough to consider."

I pause again. Even Idris seems impressed.

"I would like to analyse this manuscript here in this

sanctuary. All I would require are a few instruments that I can easily arrange to be transported here if necessary. I imagine the work can be completed in about a week. Once I am done, I will share my findings with you, and return to Oxford. The manuscript would remain here, of course, for you to preserve in your archives or at the *Biblioteca Apostolica Vaticana*, or, if you so wish, to share in a public exhibition."

My use of Italian, which, like my Portuguese, I only have a working knowledge of, did not go unnoticed. The cardinal straightens his back and begins to nod his head in silence. I have left an unmistakable impression on him, and even his suspicious nun seems to be now on my side.

He is speaking to me directly now, perhaps convinced that I understand his Portuguese, though I am only able to catch a few words. I wait for the nun to share her interpretation:

"The truth you shared is appreciated. I believe it to be the truth. I believe your presence here is part of a divine plan to help us understand better the secrets of the Lady of Fátima."

I smile often to express agreement with his patriarchal, self-serving bullshit.

"You can begin your work tomorrow. We will prepare everything. Your belongings and transport will be moved here from the hotel. You will be our guests until your work is done. I only ask that the cylinder does not leave the Sanctuary. Never leaves the Sanctuary."

Those last words were uttered with stronger emphasis. It is clear that the only point that would not include compromise of any sort is the removal of the cylinder from the premises.

"Yes, of course, your Eminence. The cylinder will always remain here."

He smiles and reaches his hand towards me in a manner that first makes me think he wants me to shake it. Then, I realise he's expecting me to place something in it. And here I was thinking I would at least be able to spend all night examining the scroll. I reluctantly reach for my bag and place the cylinder in his hand. He stares at it in awe, and then places it carefully on the coffee table between us. Now I'm angry though I'm careful not to show it. Pam Grier, black and sensationally powerful, arrives at the scene. She's carrying a rifle which she points at everyone, as she repeats one of her iconic lines:

"This is the end of your rotten life, you mother-fuckin' dope pusher."

Everyone is shot repeatedly and blood splatters everywhere. She places the cylinder in her pocket and lights a cigarette before leaving the scene.

The polished me stands up and smiles as Idris and I are led by the nun to our respective rooms. It's been a long day, and I fall asleep imagining Khatia Buniatishvili's breasts bounce as she violently plays Schumann's Piano Concerto in A Minor.

(10)

I dream it's 2009 all over again. The year of *Mowj-e-Sabz*, the Green Wave that overwhelmed the streets of Iran and made me for once proud of my father's roots. In my dream, as was the case in real life, I was in Damascus on a foreign exchange program. I'm standing at the point where the souk ends, under the remains of the Roman entrance to the Temple of Jupiter. Across from me should be the Grand Mosque, but instead there is a gigantic screen showing the women of Iran carrying the slogan, 'Where is my vote?' The camera zooms in on the face of a young woman who is as beautiful as she is proud. She believes, and her faith flows like a river from Tehran to Damascus. Suddenly, men in black turbans arrive. A guillotine is hurriedly set up and women are led up, one by one, on the scaffold, and forced to kneel. The hatchet descends with violent force, and heads are decapitated. Beautiful proud heads roll down and quickly form a pyramid of bitter death. Suddenly, God arrives wearing a blue headscarf and a navy coat. With my eyes still fixed on the screen, I murmur, "Why don't you do something? Stop this or I swear I will never speak to you again." She answers, even as her eyes, too, remain focused on the screen, "Speak to me? When did you ever speak to me?" I wake up with my heart beating like a drum.

I stand and inhale the steam. The shower cubicle is small, like everything else in this room, but the water is hot–hot enough to erase the scenes of my dream. My hand moves below, but I'm not inspired, just tense, bordering on angry. All of this is so awkward. What the hell am I doing in a building that belongs to the Catholic church? A medieval institution that once inspired the Crusades and oversaw the Spanish Inquisition. Why am I willing to depart so far from my comfort zone? What the fuck possessed me to jump on a plane to Lisbon? A pathetic hope that this scroll could somehow be the antidote to all the poison with which my faith has been injected? As though this scroll will change anything, can change anything. As though anything is capable of changing anything at this point in my life. I have lost my faith; it was guillotined in the streets of Tehran, and all that remains of it is a headscarf which, like the remains of the Temple of Jupiter, is a relic of what was, rather than a manifestation of what is.

There's a knock at my door. It's Idris saying something about breakfast. I ignore him and focus on the pleasure I am experiencing walking around naked and wet in my room. It feels like a sweet form of desecration. Something neither the cardinal nor his penguin would approve of. I stare at the mirror, and now the inspiration finally arrives. I lie on the bed with Christopher Atkins, a far more delicious breakfast than anything Idris is having. He's as young as he was in *The Blue Lagoon*, or maybe a bit younger. I whisper in his ear, "I want you to pretend you are asleep." I blow on each of his eyes, and they close like magic. He's already naked, and so am I. I sit over him and guide him inside me. This is no doubt my favourite position. Not only does it give me all the control I crave, but it allows me to quickly go on the offensive if my boys decide to misbehave. Sure enough, and in clear violation of my express desire, Chris opens his eyes, and I slap him; first gently, but then with force. "Don't do that again." His cheeks go red, and he complies. Three orgasms later, I'm finally ready for breakfast and scenes of nuns and priests.

I climb down the steps and follow the sounds to a large dining room with several tables. I find Idris chatting away with the interpreting penguin. There's a large platter of cheese, which like everything else in this place, is named after a saint, in this case Saint Jorge. The penguin explains that it's a very special cheese that is aged in the caves of the Azores Mountains. There's also bread, large and rustic, and a jug of orange juice. But all of this is meaningless to me. My eyes are only interested in locating coffee. I need at least one cup for each orgasm, and at this point I'm three cups short. Idris appears to have some basic intuition and he interrupts the nun to tell me where I can find coffee. He points at one of the corners of the room, and I'm literally ready to shout 'Hallelujah!' when I spot a large electric percolator. It looks like it belongs to a mid-century vintage collection, but the stainless-steel shines as though it was taken out of its box just this morning. I pour the black gold into my cup and hold it with both hands, as a mother would hold her child. "Okay," I whisper to myself, "I can do this now."

The interpreting penguin turns out to have a name: Maria. Sister Maria informs me that Cardinal Saraiva is waiting for me along with other important Vatican officials in the conference room. He would like me to make a small presentation before I start examining the scroll.

"Maybe you can make a presentation at each morning? Maybe you can cover a subject related to your research and expertise? That would be most appreciated."

I nod in agreement, as I silently answer her, "Maybe you can just give me the scroll, and let me get on with my fucking life!" Idris, the intuitive, shows up and decides to share his wisdom.

"Don't let them provoke you. As long as they let us examine the scroll, they can have everything they want."

He senses the obscenities I silently select for him and moves out of my way.

(11)

I follow Maria the Penguin as she leads me in and out of narrow corridors and finally to spiral stairs that she quickly climbs down. I know Idris is a few steps behind me. And suddenly, for some pathetic, undoubtedly oestrogen-related impulse, it's actually comforting to know that he's coming along. I find myself in an auditorium full of men in black cassocks and white masks. Carly Simon starts singing in my head:

"You walked into the party
Like you were walking on to a yacht.
Your hat strategically dipped below one eye,
Your scarf, it was apricot."

You may have noticed that I'm not often in a good mood—and that, as my mother would say, my go-to feeling is anger. But this morning I am particularly pissed. I have travelled, under very severe conditions, all the way from Mansfield College in Oxford, risked my professional reputation, and agreed to sleep in a Catholic sanctuary of all places, only for these men in black to decide to have me prostitute my academic self before they deign to allow me to examine the scroll I am here to see. And so, I decide that it's time to strip these men of their self-serving, historically groundless beliefs. Look, they asked for it. I was more than willing to live and let live. But they clearly wanted more. So, more they will get.

"Good morning, everyone. I must say I am honoured by this opportunity to give the first of several presentations I hope to share with you on various subjects related to the discovery of a scroll in the Castle of Ourém."

Never mind that I don't know what the fuck is in that scroll. Never mind that these theology addicts have probably never been exposed to the historical method.

"I would like to emphasise that what I will share with you today is purely based on academic research and I apologise in advance if it in any way is regarded by you as uncomfortable or offensive."

Penguin Maria is standing two meters or so to my right and is energetically interpreting my words. I can see Idris sitting in the back row. And again, I find myself liking the idea that he's there. The masks the cardinals and priests are wearing make it hard for me to capture impressions as I speak. I was never an eye person. Eyes give out too much information about an individual that I am simply not interested in. I would rather focus on smiles, lip-pursing, and the various other types of mouth gymnastics that provide me with all the information I need.

"You must all be familiar with the legend of Princess

Fátima, for which this city is famous, and after which this sanctuary is named."

I pause for a few seconds to make sure that Maria had actually used the word *'lenda'*. I did not want this specific word to be moderated. And I am pleased to hear her pronounce it, though I do sense a hint of discomfort.

"This legend was transmitted to us by Friar Bernardino de Brito. Friar Brito is the author of the Chronicle of the Order of Cister, a work he completed in 1602. It is in this work that we find the earliest record of the legend of Fátima, with all its important elements that were destined over time to be embellished and dramatised. Even Robert Southey, an English poet and one of the Romantics, was inspired by the work of Brito to write a poem which he named after Gonzalo Hermiguez, a larger-than-life knight and warrior who allegedly fought under Alfonso Henriquez. So famous was Gonzalo for his successful raids against the Moors that he was known, according to Brito, as *Traga Mouros*, or 'the Moor Eater'."

The penguin apparently finds this humorous and lets slip a snort.

"But Gonzalo was not merely a blood-thirsty warrior, he was also, we are informed by Brito, a poet. In fact, some of the verses ascribed to him are said to be the oldest in the Portuguese language. According to Brito's legend, Gonzalo and his fellow warriors raided the town Alcacer do Sal and managed to kidnap Princess Fátima, a Moorish Muslim woman who was so charmed by the Moor Eater that she agreed to renounce her religion, be baptised, and marry him, and live with her husband until her death in the town in which we stand today. And though the legend is careful to mention that Fátima acquired the Christian name of Ouriana upon her baptism, we are informed that the town adopted her original Muslim name as its own."

I pause for a few seconds before I deliver my knockout blow.

"Sadly, and I say sadly because I like everyone else have a weakness for legends, this story belongs entirely to the Christian lore of the Reconquista. As several scholars, including, most notably, Moisés Espírito Santo, sociology professor at the New University of Lisbon, have pointed out the town of Fátima was known by this name long before our friend the Moor Eater was said to have been active. This area—in fact the entire region of Sierra d'Aire—was known to be the location of what might be described as a cult of Fatima, the daughter of the Prophet of Islam. Towns with Arabic or Islamic names are quite common in both Portugal and Spain. Not too far from here, for example, is a town by the name of 'Meca' where the beautiful Church of Santa Quitéria de Meca is located. Another town named Fátima can also be found in Spain. Many of these towns have similar legends that attempt to explain why the Arabic names persisted. But the explanations, I am afraid, are far more likely to be based on the historical fact that the Arabs were here for centuries, than they are on the legends associated with the battles that evicted them."

In other words, their entire story is bullshit. I restrained myself from asking whether they've given any thought to the reason why the Virgin Mary would, allegedly, appear three times in 1917 to a group of children in the only town in the country named after the daughter of the Prophet of Islam? But my mother's words come back to me: 'If you can't say anything nice, don't say anything at all.'

A stillness takes over the entire auditorium. I can sense their desire to queue up and take turns at slapping my face for daring to question the very legend upon which this sanctuary was built. But Carly Simon is back, singing in my head, and I am completely indifferent to all the discomfort I have clearly inflicted upon them.

Suddenly, one of the men in black stands up. He addresses Maria as though I am invisible to him. Maria interprets:

"Father Faria would like to enquire from you regarding a story he has read about *Mokhamed*.

In this story, Mokhamed forces a Jewish woman to marry him after he has killed her father and her husband. His Eminence would like to know if this story is also a legend."

You bastard. Is this what they teach at the seminary? To shit-sling in response to academic research?

"Thank you, your Eminence, for your question. I believe you are referring to the Battle of Khaybar, which Muhammad, the Prophet of Islam, fought against the Jews who had decided to side with the polytheists against the newly founded Muslim community. In the spirit of many biblical figures, like David and Solomon, Muhammad was not only a religious guide; he was also the political and military leader of his community. And also, like many of the biblical patriarchs, the Prophet of Islam was indeed also married to several women."

Should I or should I not remind him of David's marriage to Bathsheba? A bona fide Biblical version of what he's insinuating.

"What I find fascinating about the story you make reference to is precisely the fact that it does not lend itself to those elements we generally associate with legends. Firstly, it is indeed found in early Islamic sources, and secondly, it is not whitewashed. This woman, whose name was Safiyya, in the same sources that contain the story of her marriage to the Prophet, informs us how much she hated Muhammad when she first met him on the night after the battle, and how long he spent apologizing and explaining to her what had taken place between the Muslims and her Jewish tribe. Neither her grief nor her anger is omitted. Decades after the Prophet's death, we know that Safiyya—far from being damaged and withdrawn—was, in fact, willing to risk her life in support of a political position which few Muslims endorsed at the time. By contrast, at no point in Brito's account of the story of Fátima do we hear her voice; the voice of a woman who had been kidnapped, taken from her family and friends, and was now married to a man with whom she did not even share a language. The story of Safiyya may appear uncomfortable to our modern sensibilities, but it is not a fairy tale."

I could swear I hear someone clapping, and sure enough, I can see Idris in the back row, with a beaming grin giving me a one-man standing ovation, his floppy black fringe falling into his eyes. It appears my words have thankfully discouraged any further questions. I watch everyone file out and I wait impatiently, my mind fixated on what I have been waiting all morning for. Idris approaches the podium and mumbles some crap about how much he appreciated my presentation. Something in me believes him, but I'm instantly aware that I'm uncomfortable with that something.

Maria finally returns, looking nervous.

"On behalf of Cardinal Saraiva, I would like to apologise because it will not be possible to examine the scroll today."

"I beg your pardon?"

"Some preparations have not been finalised. By tomorrow morning everything will be ready."

I have to leave. I know that if I don't leave, my Persian genes will kick in and instead of having to deal with an Oxford professor, Maria and her friends will suddenly be faced with raw Middle Eastern rage. My hand, almost by reflex, slides into my pocket and clutches my car keys.

(12)

I'm heading west. I have an overwhelming desire to immerse myself in water. Using the satnav, I map out a straight line from Fátima all the way to the Atlantic Ocean. My destination is Pataias, a beach town about 28 miles from Ourém. I find myself desperate for air, even though the top is down. I drive faster, inviting the wind to blow straight into my face. My playlist is streaming through the Fiat's speakers, and Dariush is singing *Age Ye Rooz*. I turn it up, until the sounds of Persian music and the wind blast against the fabric over my ears. I am trying to drown out the voices in my head. If I must have this conversation, I do not want to have it here.

Forty minutes later, I reach Rainha Santa Isabel, a curved road with parking spaces to the left of the bend. I spot a steep path leading from the tarmac, and I climb down quickly. Perhaps it's the time of day, or perhaps it's one of the few gifts of corona, but the beach is entirely empty. Though in the state of mind I'm in, I'm not sure it would have mattered had it not been.

I take off my sandals. My black trousers. My silver shirt. My white pants and bra. I reach for my scarf and I hesitate. How strange it is that even now the hardest thing for me to remove is my headscarf. I put my satchel on top of my clothes to weigh them down. At least there's something in me still thinking rationally.

The first thing I notice is the feeling of the breeze now blowing directly against my ears. Next, I notice my breasts and the strange awareness of open-air freedom, to which my nipples instantly react. I have long felt that the idea it is okay in western secular society for men to walk around shirtless, even as women are actually arrested for doing the same, is a relic of a medieval past that our patriarchal lenses are unable to shed. Mind you, who am I to speak, when I go around covering not only my breasts but my hair too?

I run to the water, and I'm glad when my feet register just how cold it is. I plunge in, purposely keeping my eyes open. I am hungry for the painful sensations of cold water and salty stings. But they are not enough. I need a dose of fear. I want to scare my head into silence. So, I swim. Away from the shore. I swim far enough to be aware that I could easily become a news item in tomorrow's papers: 'Oxford professor ignores dangerous currents—swept out to sea'. I take all of this in—the temperature, the salt in my eyes, the panic setting in. I head back to the beach.

Sat huddled by my clothes, I reach into my satchel and, still shivering, rummage around for my packet of American Spirits—organic, additive-free cigarettes that are guaranteed to kill you only in the healthiest possible way. A few years ago, I made the decision that I am allowed to smoke only when nothing else has helped me breathe. I inhale North Carolina's finest, and exhale the smoke against my wet, sandy feet.

Now finally, I am ready for the conversation I have avoided ever since Father Faria decided to assault me with his remark about Safiyya. Little did he know that Safiyya belongs to a long list of topics that my tutors at Oxford, years ago, decided to indulge in through what was meant to be an introductory course on Islamic History. Professor Tuttle had clearly had a fetish for all things exotic and vulgar, especially when they appeared to involve–directly or indirectly–the Prophet. And so there I was, a nineteen-year-old Muslim woman, proud and flowing with faith, suddenly being forced to confront stories that implied that the man in whom I had had unconditional faith was charged–in the vainglorious, tendentious courts of western academia–with acts of lust, violence, war crimes, and even genocide. Safiyya and the Battle of Khaybar were high on that list which Tuttle had been so fond of mentioning in his Wednesday morning lectures.

My initial reaction then had been to run to my father for consolation. After all, in my mind he was responsible for sowing the seeds of my religion and was therefore responsible for defending it. My mother–a convert–was the spiritual one, and was neither able to relate to these subjects, nor did she seem in any way affected by them. In contrast to my father, her faith derived neither energy nor challenge from religious debates. When eventually my father's comforting responses stopped working, my deep and intensive research had begun. This is where it gets complicated. Because while it was clear to me that the underlying logic of Tuttle and his cronies—which claimed that it was possible to use our modern, even post-modern, values and sensibilities to evaluate the behaviour and actions of a man who lived in seventh century Arabia—was flawed, I still wanted this man, my Prophet, to pass this test on their terms. There was still something within me, a spiritual innocence, or perhaps desperation, that wanted the Prophet to emerge from these stories untainted. And even though the very sources that contained the stories Tuttle was addicted to sharing also contained words and actions that were more often incredibly kind and gracious—which of course Tuttle consistently ignored—I had continued to hope that I would discover, through my own research, a way to convincingly prove that none of the uncomfortable incidents had ever happened. I never did.

And so, as I take a last draw on my cigarette, I decide to ask him directly. Something I'd never dared to do.

"Did it not occur to you that a day would come when a young woman who thought the world of you would have to listen to some pathetic, stuck up, self-righteous orientalist lecture her about what you did at Khaybar? Couldn't you just have marched back? What difference would it have made? What am I supposed to say to these people? What would you want me to say to them? Forget them, who cares about them? What about me? What do I say to this voice in my head? To whom do you leave me?"

(13)

I dream I'm walking down St. Clement's, a road that runs between my home—in the 'ghetto' part of town—and the High Street. It is the road of my childhood. It knows me as well as I know it. The tall girl with the white headscarf, the light complexion, and the deep Persian eyes. I know the shops by heart. I could write a book about how they have changed over the years—the ones that began as restaurants and ended up as charity shops, and the few that managed to survive as they were. My school, just off the main road, a shitty establishment threatened multiple times with government closure, celebrated me as its only student to have ever applied to, let alone be accepted at Oxford.

I walk into a shop that sells perfume. And I'm not surprised that God is the shopkeeper. She is standing on the other side of the counter, once again dressed in a navy coat and blue headscarf. She is holding a small bottle of perfume and she beckons me to smell. I am hit by the first burst of scent—something reminiscent of rosewater and musk, the second burst is reminiscent of jasmine, and the third of warm sandalwood. She says to me, "These are the scents of the man to whom you were speaking." I want to reply but no words come to me. I want to scream, "But what about Safiyya?"

She looks into my eyes and answers, "You think it was me who told him to?"

Again, I wake up with my heart beating like a drum.

(14)

My rape fantasies began when I was around 14. So much about them is vague and mysterious. I've often wondered what a therapist would have done with these. Or even what Sabina Spielrein or Carl Jung would have made of my imaginings. Why would anyone experience pleasure visualizing an event that they would be willing to die to avoid in real life? My own personal theory is that it has to do with being mentally violated. Something must have happened, somewhere in my childhood, that made me feel so uncomfortable mentally, something that violated my most basic expectation of rational behaviour in others, that it unleashed in me the desire to expunge my sense of being trampled on via an experience of physical violation.

Psycho-analytic bullshit aside, I wake up with the desire to replay one of these scenes. The urge is intense and irresistible. I close my eyes and let it take over me. Faceless men—now in cassocks—storm into my room and take turns violating me in every conceivable fashion. I resist, but only enough to intensify the experience. My orgasm is stretched, drawn out and deep, and I am left immobile, as though I've been hit by a sledgehammer.

I am certain of one only thing: I must see that scroll.

In the dining hall, I find Maria again speaking to Idris. It is clear they were worried about my disappearance yesterday. Perhaps they were even worried that I would not have returned at all. I walk towards them confidently and, focusing all my attention on my next words, I say, in Portuguese, "Before there can be any further presentations, I must see the scroll." Maria is startled—my intended effect—clearly surprised to be addressed in her own language, though in my mind my pronunciation was far from perfect. She disappears, returning a few minutes later, and finds me inhaling my second cup of coffee.

"His Eminence has agreed you are now welcome to examine the scroll. The seminar room has been completely prepared."

I place my cup on the nearest table and rush out of the room. Maria quickly follows me and mumbles something to the effect that she will show me where the seminar room is. Idris catches up with me, looking like he's about to have a heart attack. I ignore him. I simply cannot understand what possible motive lies behind his intense interest in all this—other than writing some stupid article in some cheap, worthless magazine.

We climb one flight of stairs. Maria leads us to a room

with a large table in the middle. On it are arranged several antiquated instruments, which would be considered fit only for a museum back home. But they'll have to do. Just as I'm about to approach the table, Maria taps my arm. She makes the KGB-style demand for our mobile phones. They clearly do not want any more pictures of the manuscript to be taken. For God's sake. We hand them over. Next, Maria produces two forms from a folder under her arm and asks each of us to sign one. Idris reads quickly and signs his name. Though I'm anxious to get started on the scroll, I read through the form carefully. I'm not in the habit of signing church contracts without checking them first. It turns out to be an agreement asking us to adhere to the cardinal's conditions. I sign, and hand the paper back to Maria, who takes a key from her pocket, unlocks a metal case in the middle of the table, and lifts the lid.

As she does so, the light from the soft electric lamp bent over the box catches the silver cylinder, and it glows. Finally. Maria takes her leave, firmly closing the seminar room door behind her.

I am pleased to see pairs of cotton gloves laid out. I gesture to Idris to put them on, before he does anything stupid like try and open it with his bare hands.

The outside of the cylinder is plain, and though this would have to be tested, my initial guess is that the metalwork does not date back to earlier than the twelfth century.

I now reach into the box and pick up the cylinder. Using my gloved hands, I take hold of both ends and twist, pulling gently. Idris is standing far too close to me, hovering over my shoulder. It is easy to open, perhaps because Idris's neighbour had loosened it not too long ago. With the two metal parts detached, I tip the cylinder so that the contents slide onto the equipment. I am surprised to find not one but two small pieces of parchment, tightly rolled, one inside the other. I gingerly unroll the outer parchment, spreading it over the glass plate of the machine in front of me, and use the clips to gently fasten it in place. I take a few seconds and remind myself to breathe. I pull the magnifier towards me, positioning it over the manuscript.

Idris is the first to speak, "What on earth?" For once, our sentiments align.

At the top of the page, I recognise the words from the photograph that Idris had sent in his initial email. I had correctly identified it to read:

On the authority of The Blossoming One

And below these words was the image of a hand.

A right hand, palm-up, is depicted, as though

someone had perhaps stencilled around their own. On each of the fingers are three different words, with a further two on the thumb. Fourteen in total. Below the image, names have been listed in three columns, with a fourth column left blank. The seventh century Hijazi lettering I recognised from the words at the top of the page is only evident on the hand itself. The names, however, judging from the differing styles of the script, and the varying colours of the ink, have been added incrementally, apparently by multiple authors. Signatures of some sort.

I unroll the second scroll. This, I can tell, is more recent. Like the cylinder, my guess is that this is also early Middle Ages. With clips in place, I once again pause for breath.

"It looks like that stone they found, what was it called? The one they used to decipher the hieroglyphics." He's right, it does resemble the Rosetta Stone, though I say none of this aloud.

This page begins with Arabic. Below it is Latin. At the bottom, Hebrew. Several lines each. My quick glance at the Arabic tells me it's some kind of prayer. But not one with which I am remotely familiar.

I take a step back and allow my eyes to absorb the scene. This is far more than I was expecting, though in truth I don't know what I had been expecting at all.

(16)

I spend hours hunched over the manuscripts, examining, slowly focused on replicating the image and carefully transcribing and translating each word. I've lost track of time entirely, I ignore the growing stiffness in my neck and shoulders, the ache in my eyes.

Idris has made himself useful by replenishing my coffee supplies. He had eventually realised, after multiple failed attempts, that I was not planning to answer any of his questions. I have too many of my own. Foremost of which concerns the number fourteen. Where else is this important?

I have come across several outlandish works in the past claiming to have identified the numerical miracle of the Quran, but these are usually obsessed with the number nineteen. Far more interesting works by al-Buni and Ibn 'Arabi, both thirteenth century Muslim mystics and philosophers, were preoccupied by the number seven—seven heavens, seven days of the week, seven archangels. But nothing I've ever read has emphasised the number fourteen.

I make the possibly unwise decision that the ideal way to ensure Idris is entirely out of my hair, so to speak, is to actually ask for his help.

"Could you do me a favour? This is clearly going to take some time for me to read and decipher. In the meantime, it would be really helpful if you could research whether the number fourteen is mentioned anywhere in Islamic literature. Any possible reference would be useful."

He seems only too eager to finally be given something meaningful to do. Since we had not been allowed to bring our laptops into the room either, Idris returned to his room to use the internet there, leaving me, finally, alone.

I turn my attention back to the parchments. The Hijazi script has no dots or diacritical markings, so individual words could have a number of possible interpretations—I systematically make a note of all of them. Interestingly, I notice, the letters at the beginning of each word seem to be significantly darker, bolder almost, than the rest of the letters. This may just be the scribe's style. I make a note of it, nonetheless.

In my focus on the individual words, I am constantly drawn back to the feeling that these must be linked—they represent a larger, unified whole. This isn't just a list of random items, it's a diagram. Of what, though? A blueprint? A map?

But I need all the pieces to figure out this puzzle. I go back to transcribing and translating.

Five hours later, I finally arrive at my first draft. I add question marks or alternate possible readings when I'm not sure of what I've arrived at:

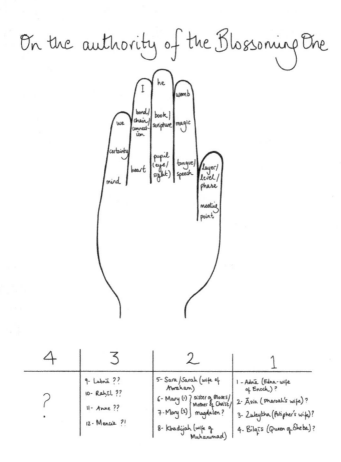

On the authority of the Blossoming One

4	3	2	1
?	9- Lubnā ??	5- Sara /Sarah (wife of Abraham)	1 - Adnā (Edna- wife of Enoch) ?
	10- Raḥīl ??	6- Mary (i) ⎫ sister of Moses/ mother of Christ/	2- Āsia (Pharaoh's wife) ?
	11- Anne ??	7- Mary (ii) ⎭ magdalen ?	3- Zuleykha (Potipher's wife)?
	12- Mencia ?!	8- Khadijah (wife of Muhammad)	4- Bilqīs (Queen of Sheba) ?

I have no intention of stopping. How can I possibly take a break before examining the second manuscript? I'm far too afraid that if I leave this room, I'll be told for some new ridiculous reason that I won't be able to come back in again. I'm not taking that risk. My bladder can wait.

I turn to the second scroll. This promises to be an easier task. I'm far more familiar with the Andalusian script. I've spent half my life at Oxford studying Arabic manuscripts from Muslim Spain. It takes about two hours to transcribe and translate it.

In each corner of this parchment, three words are inscribed. I assume, given the Arabic script, that these should be read anticlockwise, top to bottom. Following this logic, they read:

Who gazes, dies - who dies, sees - who sees, was - who was, becomes.

Gazes upon what though? This scroll? What on earth does it contain? This apparent warning does nothing to deter me from turning now to the text in the middle of the page. Though I will double check this later, I have enough knowledge of Latin and Hebrew to surmise that they are exact or very close translations of the Arabic, which I focus on deciphering:

يا نار وأمان

يا دمار وقرآن

يا سر الإنسان

يا نحن الأكوان

طواف ولدان

ثوب سلطان

نبيذ رمان

خاتم العرفان

O ignis O praesidium
O exitium O scripturae
O humanum secretum
O nos universi

Tribue nobis cælestium iuvenum congregationem
involve nos in auctoritatis togis
extingue sitem nostram malogranato vino
Large nobis perfectum anulum scientiae.

הוֹי אש הוֹי מחסה
הוֹי הרס הוֹי כתבי קודש
אוֹי סוד האדם
הוֹי אנן דיקוּמא
תן לנוּ כינוּס נערים שמימיים
עטף אותנו בטליתות סמכות
שבענו ביין רימונים
טבעת הדעת השלמה שים עלינו

O Fire, O Protection,
O Destruction, O Scripture,
O Secret of the Human,
O We of the Cosmos,

[Grant us] a gathering of heavenly youths;
[Enrobe us in] gowns of authority;
[Quench us with] pomegranate wine;
[Bestow upon us] the seal/ring of knowledge
complete.

Is this addressing... God? If so, it appears to do so in four distinctive and peculiar ways, then proceeds to ask for four different things. Like the words of the hand, I can't help but feel that there is something more here, a message of some sort that underlies the words of this invocation.

I walk out of the seminar room, like Lazarus emerging from the cave. I am starving in ways that are hard to describe. My bladder is about to explode. But most prominent of all is the pain in my head. I stumble into Maria, who is heading down the corridor towards me. She clearly wants to talk. I can't. I wave and head quickly in the direction of my room.

Idris, hearing me jamming the key into my lock, emerges from the room next to mine.

"I need two things: paracetamol—the strongest you can find—and chocolate."

I don't wait for his response. I barely have time to pull down my trousers in the bathroom. I remember being told by Mrs Dales, my primary school teacher, that I would do damage to my bladder if I held in my pee for too long. I hated those school toilets. The doors were too short, and teachers would come in to check on you. I found the entire experience insulting, even at six. So far though, no damage has been done, though on this occasion I'm not so sure.

Empty and relieved, I crash onto the bed, too tired to have even taken off my shoes. Everything hurts, but my head most of all. The pain, acute and hot, radiates from my shoulders all the way to the back of my eyes.

I must have drifted off though, because I am startled awake by a persistent knocking on the door. In too much pain to move, I call out, "It's open."

Idris walks in, slowly and cautiously. He approaches the bed and puts a packet of painkillers in my hand.

"Food first."

He takes out a bar of chocolate from the carrier bag he's brought with him. I rip open the packaging and take two large bites. There's a strong taste of artificial strawberry. It's revolting, but I need the sugar and I'm too desperate to complain. He hands me a large glass bottle of water. I down half the contents and knock back three tablets with another swig. He mumbles, "I think you're only supposed to take two…" I ignore him. I lie back down, expecting him to leave. I don't hear him move.

"I think I found something… Something about fourteen."

I sit up slowly, and exhale. I reach for my notes, mostly as a gesture of graciousness to the guy who just brought me pain relief, though most of me is convinced that what he's about to share will be crap.

"You know how the Quran has mysterious letters at the beginning of some of its chapters? Well, it turns out that, even though they appear in various repetitive combinations, the actual number of individual letters used is fourteen."

I physically feel the thought forming in my brain. Fourteen words, fourteen letters. There might be something here…

"Tell me the letters."

He takes out a piece of paper from his pocket and starts reading.

"Wait. One by one."

He starts again: "*Alif.*"

There it is: "*Ana* – 'I'."

"*Lam.*"

"*Lisan* – Tongue, speech."

"*Meem.*"

"*Majma'* – Meeting place."

'Ra."

"Rahm – Womb."

"Sad."

"Silah – Connection."

" 'Ayn."

" 'Aql – Mind."

"Kaf."

"Kitab – Scripture."

"Ya."

"Yaqeen – Certainty."

"Ta."

"Tabaq – Sphere, level."

"Ha."

"Huwa – He."

"Seen."

"Sihr – Magic."

"Ḥa."

"Ḥadaqah – Pupil."

"Qaf."

"Qalb – Heart."

"Nun."

"Nahnu – We... Oh my God, we fucking cracked it."

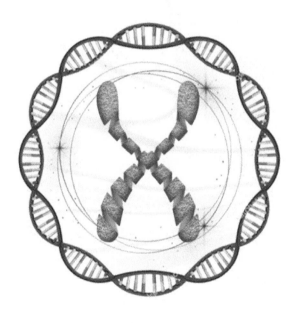

(17)

We can share stories, numerous stories, of two bodies—hopelessly attracted, sexually aroused—surrendering to their passions, and becoming, if only for a few seconds, physically one. Alas, physical unity is quickly replaced with sweat and discomfort. Awkwardness follows, and what was 'one' quickly becomes vividly 'two'. Questions arise. Was he as willing to pleasure me as I was him? Didn't she realise that I wanted her to vocalise her ecstasy? The answers, invariably negative, replace the mystery of physical discovery with a geography tainted by flags and borders. At this point, the fantasy is either domesticated, or the maps are torn up, the unity dissolves, and a new quest is initiated.

We can also share stories of overwhelming love. Marriage, or a common shared life of some sort, the frequent destination for most of these stories, has a way of shattering this particular type of emotional unity. And so, the longing to see her, the anticipation of his arrival, the sweetness of being lost in another person's eyes—all this is replaced by watching the same person over and over again lying on the couch and fiddling with his phone. You were once his singular focal point of attention. You once dreamt of a common destination, now you are at best a passenger in a plane which he is flying solo. What was 'one' has become ruthlessly 'two' again.

Watch with Us the most surreal manifestation of this type of bond. A couple celebrating their sixtieth anniversary. What have they not survived? What do they not know about each other? You walk into their home expecting to see the perfect embodiment of marital bliss, but instead you are witness to an endless stream of bickering. Bitter and spiteful words are exchanged over something as trivial as where socks were left, or why the toilet seat is still up. Where bickering is not now the new normal, chances are you will instead walk into walls of silence, heavy with disappointment, permeated with memories of promises broken, expectations unmet, or worse, forgotten.

Far less common are stories of mental unity. What exactly happens when brains–the organs that appear to capture the very awareness of individuality–blend into each other in a rare moment of mutual recognition? Where does this lead? How long can it last?

Such was the moment, the second, when Fatima and Idris suddenly realised that they had identified fourteen words that perfectly corresponded with the fourteen mysterious–and as of yet impossible to decode–letters of the Quran. She had indeed asked him to leave shortly after this discovery. But even as she lay back down, waiting for her body, her head, to respond to the painkillers, it was clear to her that something entirely unexpected–and so surprisingly new—had just taken place. And as Idris walked back to his room, he also realised that he had finally been promoted to a man Fatima was willing to see. Not as someone she was trying to avoid, nor someone who could perform some meaningless service, nor as someone who was eternally guilty of various patriarchal sins. Not even as a man, but as a mind.

As he undressed and got into his pyjamas, he noticed that his body had found this experience inexplicably arousing. There was something incredibly enticing about what had just taken place between them, but it was far removed from the realm of his Playmates, or his Portuguese neighbour. And he was as embarrassed as he was thrilled at this thought.

(18)

Fatima had awoken with a plan brewing. She dressed quickly and headed down to the dining hall. Surveying the room, she quickly identified the man she was looking for. She strode over to Idris and handed him the piece of paper. This was step one. Step two involved Maria. Fatima found her sipping tea and talking to one of the innumerable priests inhabiting the sanctuary.

"Sister Maria, I spent yesterday researching the scroll, and I believe I'm ready to share my findings in a final presentation before I must bid you farewell. I'm afraid my commitments at Oxford sadly do not permit me to extend my stay further."

Maria seemed surprised but pleased. Like the cardinal, and everyone else in the sanctuary, she had regarded the scroll as an event to be 'dealt with' swiftly and discreetly, before such an 'incident' could develop into a 'scandal'. Everything was treated as a potential scandal, part of a larger conspiracy against the church.

Fatima's presentation was brief, and primarily focused on the second of the two parchments, the first she dismissed as a medieval incantation against the evil eye. This was step three of her plan: to detract any attention from the importance and value of the hand scroll, which she had slipped in amongst her own papers the previous day. In its stead she had left a tightly rolled page of the one of the many Bibles that had lined the shelves of the examination room.

The cardinal's profuse thanks at the end of her presentation reflected the intense relief he clearly felt upon the realisation of the seemingly benign contents of the scroll. It contained nothing more than a drawing of a medieval talisman, and a harmless prayer in Arabic, Latin, and Hebrew. If anything, in the cardinal's mind, the latter represented an opportunity for the church to emphasise its ecumenical stand, which he was already at that moment planning to exploit through an interfaith event at the sanctuary in the post-coronavirus age, to which he made a mental note to invite Fatima.

Already packed and ready to leave, Fatima located Maria by the door of the auditorium to request the return of her mobile phone, passport and identification, all of which had been confiscated at various points during their brief stay. Maria, looking embarrassed, rushed to collect the items, and handed them over with a torrent of bilingual apologies.

With every nerve in her body on high alert, Fatima made her way to the entrance, flanked by Maria. She dared not breathe for fear of giving herself away at the last moment. She had calculated that her surprise departure announcement would mean that they would not have time to re-open the cylinder and check its contents until after she had left. Her calculations were correct. But not until she had climbed in the car did she finally exhale.

She sat in the Fiat, waiting for Idris to arrive. In her note, she had instructed him to drive his car to Ourém and drop it off at a branch of the rental office, and return to the sanctuary. As he pulled up in a taxi, she knew he had followed her instructions to the letter. His cooperation, without the need or request for explanation, was an extension of the experience of the night before. There was an implicit understanding of being on the same page, even though the contents of that page had not been earlier discussed.

Idris approached the car. Fatima lowered the window, "Fancy a road trip?"

That's exactly what I was hoping for."

(19)

Ourém - Guarda, Portugal (238 km)

Intrigued you must be as to who exactly We are. If you think this is just another omniscient narrator, then know that you are entirely amiss, astray, off target and off track. Firstly, this isn't fiction. What exactly does that even mean? Yet another human double-illusion. Humans are so good at that. First, they assume something they call 'real'—as unchallenging to disprove as hearts and feelings—and then they proceed to create a version of this illusion they call 'fiction'. How amusing. We watch and smile and whisper in silence: both are equally figments of your imagination. Secondly, and here you must brace yourself, We are not human. No, We are not aliens either. Nor are We some strange creature that lives under your bed. The only possible framework that will help you grasp what We are is quantum physics, though only as a very initial introduction. Think of Us as a space, a charged field of energy in which events unfold in accordance with the nature and purpose of Our very underlying design. Oh, and if you are starting to think in terms of Us being a plurality in the way in which you understand this, then, again, you are reducing Us to human constructs. We are not more than one. We are, rather, numerous manifestations of one.

We understand, none of this is intelligible to you. So, let Us then say this in the simplest possible way. We are *why* the scroll was hidden in the wall, We are *when* it was found by Fatima and Idris, and We are *how* it will be unravelled by them. Still confused? Fine, just visualise Us as the road trip they are about to embark on. The breeze that suddenly plays with her eyelashes, the rays of the sun that reflect on his lips, the restaurant in which they indulge, and, most importantly, the destination awaiting them at the end of their journey.

"So, where are we heading?" Idris asked as he threw his bag in the back and settled into the front seat.

"Nájera, once the capital of the Kingdom of Navarre. It's about seven hours northwest from here. We should arrive before sunset. I hate driving in the dark."

"As long as we are not flying, I'm happy. Who are we meeting there, exactly?"

"Doña Mencía López de Haro. I need to see the chapel where she's buried. I found the location of her tomb online, I'm hoping there might be something there to help us, maybe an inscription or an engraving."

"Mencía... the woman who was imprisoned at the tower?"

"Yes."

"I think you mentioned the tower was actually named after her?"

"Right. And if I'm correct, hers was also the final name signed under the hand. My theory is she actually wrote her name on the scroll, as though to formalise her association with whatever it is this scroll represents. I also think she was the one who hid this scroll in the tower and stencilled her own hand over the spot on the wall as a clue for someone to find it one day."

"Maybe she wanted you to find it. By the way, I'm starving. I haven't had a good breakfast since I left Southend. That Father Guilherme, the chef, was seriously overrated. The stew was good, I'll admit, but the breakfast was as bland as the sanctuary."

Fatima smiled. The person sitting next to her was a man, almost a decade older than her, of partially Arab descent, and a journalist by profession. In short, he was the last person on earth with whom she would ever have expected to be this comfortable, this mentally comfortable. He was polite, he followed instructions, he could engage in a discussion without feeling the need to make it about himself, as most men must, and, critically important, he genuinely seemed to appreciate food.

"The plan is to have a massive lunch in Guarda."

"Lunch?"

"Breakfast would mean proximity to the sanctuary, and I cannot relax until we are at least two hours away from that place."

"Understood. I fully relate. Okay, so what else do we know about Mencía?"

"Well, Mencía perfectly fits the image of a woman I'd expect to find on this scroll. She's strong, enigmatic, alluring, and hated."

"Hated?"

"Yes, wherever you find a powerful woman, you find no shortage of hateful men."

"True."

"How come you're so accepting of all of this? I can't think of a single Arab man I've met who would be."

"Neither can I. Tell me more about Mencía."

"So, she was married twice. First to Count Álvaro Pérez de Castro, and then after he died to Sancho II, King of Portugal."

"She was the Queen of Portugal?"

"Yes, but only briefly. Her first husband was much older than her. She was only thirteen when she was married to him. He, on the other hand, was already once divorced, and known for being rough, fat and ugly."

"Good job he died. Her second was the king then?"

"Right, it's said he fell madly in love with her, and some sources claim he died of grief after failing to defend her when she was kidnapped from her bedchamber."

"Wait, kidnapped?"

"Well, it appears that everyone at court was against their marriage. Why would the young king marry a widow from Castile? The idea that he was in love with her didn't help. It made him look weak, somehow susceptible to the wiles of a woman. More intriguing are the accusations of her being involved in magic and dark rituals. Eventually, the Pope issues a bull nullifying the marriage on grounds of consanguinity."

"You mean they were related?"

"Yes, her husband was something like her mother's first cousin. So anyway, against this background, troops arrive at the palace, kidnap her, and take her to Ourém where she is imprisoned in the tower. Eventually, it seems as a result of her wealth and connections, she was released, though she remained in Ourém, and even acquired land and more influence. She later moved back to Spain and is buried, in accordance with her will, at Nájera in the Benedictine convent of Santa María, in the Chapel of the Cross. Our destination."

At noon, the Fiat pulled up outside Guarda Rios. They were led by a young waiter to a table for two by a window overlooking the small waterfall and beautiful surroundings for which this restaurant was famous.

Idris took his leave to use the restroom. In the time he was gone, Fatima had scanned the menu, summoned the waiter, and, after a few brief exchanges in Portuguese, had reeled off a list of at least eight different dishes. She did not do this out of indifference to Idris, rather out of a realisation that no such socially dictated gestures were expected by him.

The first dish to arrive was *sopa de feijão com couve galega*–a soupy concoction of beans with what appeared to be kale. She had ordered along with this a plate of fried prawns and, much to Idris's delight, a large platter of cheeses.

"Fatima, did you know that sheep's cheese is high in

omega 3, and associated with longevity?"

"I did not."

"So is pomegranate wine."

"Interesting. I didn't know you drank."

"Well, the truth is I don't, but according to the Hanafi school of Islamic law, only wine from grapes is considered forbidden. Wine made of any other substance is permitted in non-intoxicating amounts."

"You're joking. A perfect example of legal gymnastics."

"That's one way to look at it. I see it more as an opportunity to have a guiltless glass of pomegranate wine every now and then."

"If only it were that simple."

Next to arrive were the three mains. *Bacalhau*, cod, breaded in this case, *Dourada do Mar*, wild sea bass grilled with lemon, and *Cabra a Nossa Moda*.

"Take your pick: cod, sea bass, or goat."

"I'm trying everything."

It's not so much what you eat, but how. The pace, the

attempt to decipher flavours, ingredients, the facial expressions, the silent conversation, the attention to each component of the dish, and the complete immersion in the experience of eating. On all these levels, there was something very much in common between them. And all of this was noticed by Fatima.

Dessert consisted of Portuguese custard, cooked in small earthenware pots, two plates of Portugal's version of rice pudding, and crackers with cheese curds and a sweet pumpkin jam. As they devoured these dishes, several espressos were requested. All this was not merely about food, though they had both clearly been extremely hungry. Something cathartic was at work here; a process of recovery from an experience that had begun at the castle and had ended only this morning.

"Did you know that American Spirits are the only additive-free, organic cigarettes in the world?"

"I did not."

"I wonder if your Hanafi school would also sanction them."

"Only if smoked with pomegranate wine."

Guarda, Portugal → Valladolid, Spain (279 km)

A Fiat, white and convertible, carrying a historian and a journalist, meandered through eastern Portugal and central Spain, past rolling green hills, and scattered villages and towns.

"Idris, do you know how to play Twenty-one Questions?"

"I think so."

"Good, well I realised that I know very little about you. So, we're playing my version."

"Go on, ask away."

"Full name?"

"Idris Jamali."

"Ancestry?"

"Syrian-British."

"That's more nationality than ancestry."

"Fine. Arab, Turkish, European, with a trace of

Ashkenazi Jewish genes."

"How could you possibly know that?"

"Easy. Two DNA tests."

"So, your mother is British?"

"Welsh, actually. And no, I can't speak Welsh."

"Interesting. Mine's English, of Dutch ancestry. So, you don't fit in anywhere either then. Okay, marital status?"

"Never married and no children."

"Technically, I didn't ask about children. Education?"

"Master's in Political Science from AUB."

"AUB? Is that an accredited university?"

"You are joking, right? The American University of Beirut is like the Oxford of the Middle East."

"I'll take your word for it. Capacity to interact with wit and sarcasm?"

"Infinite. My turn. Age?"

"Thirty-one."

"You're thirty-one and you teach at Oxford? How did that happen, exactly?"

"Well, I guess they couldn't bear the thought of me graduating and leaving them, so they hired me even before I got my PhD."

"And by 'they' you mean your colleagues at Oxford?"

"I do indeed."

"That is, I must say, impressive, and almost makes up for you not knowing about AUB. Marital status?"

"I don't believe in marriage. And the thought of having children triggers me in ways difficult to fully describe."

"Willingness to tolerate flirtatious behaviour?"

"Non-existent. Okay, Idris Jamali, now we move on to a different game. I will share a position with you, and you have to argue against it."

"Fire away."

"Okay, the Quran, as we know it, was not compiled by the Prophet Muhammad. There are no reports in which he asked for it to be compiled during his life, or even after his death. And his closest companions actually argued about whether or not it was appropriate to compile it into a book since the Prophet had not done so himself."

"I'm not sure what you think the implications are, but so far I agree."

"You agree?"

"Entirely."

"Oh. Well, most Muslims I know would be screaming by now. But I guess we've already established you're not part of that crowd."

"So, what are the implications?"

"The first possible implication is that the Quran may contain verses and even entire chapters that were private, or at least never intended to be part of a compilation that would be recited centuries later."

"Private?"

"Yes, as in verses revealed to the Prophet concerning events related to his private life, which he had recorded but which may not have been meant for the general public."

"Now that's interesting. But I still don't disagree. Does this mean that some of the Quran we recite was never intended to reach us, then?"

"It means much more than that. If you believe in all this being divinely guided—which I do—then it was purposeful for the Prophet to die before any of this was compiled. It was purposeful for it to be compiled by his companions, rather than by him."

"Purposeful how?"

"Because in this way none of it is binding and yet all of it is inspiring."

"I'm not sure I understand."

"Okay, well, think of the alternative. Imagine if the Prophet *had* left behind a fully compiled and codified, signed and sealed book—something that he could easily have done. That book would have been untouchable."

"It would be like a hard copy of God."

"Right! But this didn't happen. Although Muslims act as though it did. They even came up with these crazy philosophical arguments about whether or not the Quran was uncreated and coexistent with God."

"So, you're saying we know the Quran to be the product of some form of divine revelation, at the same time as we know it to be a result of human compilation?"

"Exactly. And that changes everything. The fact that the human element is integrated into the compilation process is a clear way of conveying the most important point here…"

"That the Quran is not God."

"Bingo!"

Only one point was missed by Fatima and Idris, a point that ensures that none of this is misunderstood as arbitrary or as reflecting a flaw in Our design. The Quran, and all scripture regarded by humans as sacred, was once seen as We intended them to be seen and are now being re-seen in the very way We intend them to be. Even as We write a new story, We weave within our very words the thread that will ultimately unravel it. Everything that is born carries within it what will ultimately cause it to die. Only We *is*–everything else *was*.

Fatima glanced over at Idris to make sure he really had understood the point. He smiled, and she smiled warmly back.

"Now, the second point relates to our scroll. Have you ever wondered why we have no reports of the Prophet explaining, or even mentioning, the mysterious letters of the Quran? Not one companion is recorded to have asked the Prophet about the meaning of these fourteen letters. We have literally thousands of reports of the Prophet's words and actions, and not a single one mentions them."

"I actually haven't. Surely, there must be a traditional explanation for this?"

"There is, or I should say, there are. Several have been proposed over the centuries. But they're all ridiculously unconvincing. The first is that the companions were too polite to ask the Prophet about these letters. That's rubbish–they asked him about everything! Another explanation is that everyone at the time already knew what they meant. Also rubbish. If they knew, we would know; it would have been recorded."

"What do Western scholars think?"

"They've also proposed some ridiculous theories. Some think the letters are abbreviations of the names of scribes. But this wouldn't explain their existence in the original compilation at all. There's no way the early companions would have allowed scribes' initials to be part of a canonised Quran. It also doesn't explain why only some of the chapters have these letters, only twenty-nine of them to be precise. And anyway, none of the scribes even have initials that correspond with these letters."

"Well, I'm lost here, because I haven't studied this in any serious way, and it was only by chance that I found out that these letters numbered fourteen. But from your tone, my feeling is you have a theory of your own."

"I do, actually. Want to hear it?"

"Absolutely. Please focus on the road though. Call me chicken, but I hate moving vehicles, especially if I'm not driving them."

"I'm going to pretend you did not just comment on my driving. Okay, here's my theory. Picture the scene: seventh century Arabia, the Prophet has passed away. His companions have argued and argued, and eventually decided that the Quran *should* be compiled into a book. Everyone was asked to produce any record of verses they had—bits they'd memorised or had written down. This included parchments from the Prophet's own home."

"His private collection?"

"Right, parts he'd asked to be written down. All of these records are brought together, cross-checked and organised. It must have been a mammoth job. Anyhow, as the people in charge are putting all this together, they notice that some of the parchments have these letters written at the beginning of certain chapters."

"Our fourteen letters."

"Exactly. Now, they've never come across these before - if they had they'd have asked the Prophet what they meant, remember?"

"Yes."

"So, what do they do? They can't remove them. They're recorded, right there in ink, and the Prophet is no longer around to be asked what should be done with them. So, they're kept."

"That's fascinating. So, we have them by the power of default?"

"Exactly, nicely put. We have them because no one had the authority to remove them. They do appear to have taught you a few things at AUB."

"Hilarious. But wait, why were they there in the first place?"

"Good question. I thought of that too. We already know the Prophet had personal scribes—people he would ask to record parts of revelation, write letters for him, treaties, things like that. My theory is that the Prophet instructed his scribes to write down these letters at the beginning of certain chapters. He didn't tell them why, and they didn't ask—that wasn't their job. Only the Prophet knew why he wanted them recorded. And they were only discovered when these parchments were found during the compilation process."

"So, it was like some sort of code that only the Prophet was aware of?"

"So I thought. But now, we might need to revise this theory."

"How come?"

"Because if our scroll really is as old as I think it is, if it really does go back to the seventh century, then this would mean there were at least some people who not only knew about these mysterious letters prior to the compilation, but also knew what they stood for. What do we know about this group of companions? Two things: first, they kept this secret; and second, they were women."

"How do you know it was only women?"

"It's obvious. There are only women's names in the columns on the scroll. And this entire manuscript begins with the words ''An al-Zahra', 'On the Authority of the Blossoming One'. Obviously, that's a reference to Fatima, the Prophet's daughter. That was her main title."

"Oh, of course! How did I miss that?"

"I suspect you also missed the fact that Fatima is said

to have had her own collection of sacred parchments, known as *Mushaf Fatima*. Of course, the Sunnis and Shi'is have been at each other's throats about this for centuries. And to this day, no one was really sure what was in it. But I have a feeling you and I just might..."

"What do you mean? And anyway, how do you know all this? I thought you were a specialist in Islamic Spain?"

"Andalusian Literature, actually. But that was just my PhD. I spent six years studying Islamic History, and almost every class I took ended up in an academic sparring match. God, if you only knew the number of times I've been asked why Islam allows wife beating. Fucking arsehole tutors."

'I usually say that's just seventh century stuff."

"Well, you'd be chewed up and spat out in about five seconds for saying that. Aren't you hungry? I'm starving."

Fatima switched on the car stereo, still connected to her phone. The first song to play was Art Garfunkel's *99 Miles to LA*. Idris closed his eyes and thought about Lynx, the cat he had abandoned in Southend.

(21)

Valladolid, Spain

In the year 705, the sixth Umayyad Caliph, Al-Walid ibn 'Abd al-Malik ibn Marwan, not a man of whom We were particularly fond, assumed rule of the Islamic empire. It was into the city of his namesake, Valladolid, City of Al-Walid, that the white Fiat now drove.

"Once we've found parking, we're looking for La Parrilla de San Lorenzo. Can you put it into your Google maps? That's assuming you're still starving?"

"I will treat that as a rhetorical question."

The restaurant, a converted sixteenth century monastery, had an unassuming exterior. But inside, Fatima and Idris felt they had been transported into a scene from a medieval castle, albeit with slightly tacky modern flourishes.

"We're here for the lamb."

They were seated beneath a renaissance depiction of an angel—sandaled of foot and trumpet in hand. Ignoring the portrait, for she had long ago filtered out all male religious iconology, Fatima reached for the menu.

"*Para empezar... queso, sopa castellana, escabechados de caza, y... chipirones y carabineros. Lechazo, obviamente. Para postre, catillas del convento, tarta de las monjas, y... el sorbete con dos cafés negros. Todo para dos personas, por favor,*" adding, in response to Idris's rather astonished expression, "I'm a specialist in Islamic *Spain*, remember?"

It is a pleasure, once again, to watch them both so immersed in the experience of eating that they become oblivious to the presence of every other person in the room.

The scent of roasted lamb arrives at the table before the dish itself. Smell is perhaps the most overlooked sense in the human experience. Sadly, humans have not yet fully understood the impact their sense of smell has on their mental and physical states. They have got as far as wondering why it is that a scent can trigger such vivid memories. How is it that you can be on a bus in Soho, smell the odour of a fellow passenger, and be transported in both time and space to somewhere you'd completely forgotten about? In the moment that the smell of oven-roasted meat hit their nostrils, the molecules at once finding their place with their appropriate savoury receptors, and at the same time strumming a rhythm of waves—a very recent human discovery—that travels their nervous systems to their brains, in that very moment, Fatima found herself at a barbeque in the back garden of her childhood home, and Idris on a beach with his parents in Latakia. Even as these scents carry them back, the aromas concurrently form new memories and associations within them, and indeed between them. If people were aware of what exactly takes place when sharing a meal with another person, they would be far more selective in their choice of culinary partners, since all of this can be as intense mentally as sexual intercourse is physically.

The hierarchy of senses is made particularly obvious with food, although We must say, more so with human intimacy. In this particular scene, the arrival of each dish—the Castilian soup, aged sheep's cheese, sauteed squid—spelled out the symphony with pristine clarity. First, the dish is spied from across the room. The sound of the sizzling becomes ever more audible, accompanied by the rhythm of footsteps and silverware, the crack of the crème brûlée, the tinkle of the sugar cube in the coffee cup. The smell arrives next, wafts and waves—fragrant, sweet, sharp, sour, earthy, rich. Then, touch—although western culinary norms have somewhat deprived humans of this component—the satisfaction of tearing bread, the running of oil down one's fingers. And then... taste. Perhaps the most intimate of all sensual experiences. Lemon sorbet with coffee. An assault of contradictory and complementary flavours, hopelessly confused.

They had decided to walk. The June Mediterranean

heat was subsiding, and the breeze outside the restaurant cooled the sweat that had formed on their skin. They walked in the direction of greenery. Of open space and water. Since it was now late afternoon, the park that had been built along the river's edge was littered with children and tired-looking parents. Everything around them was loud, but the sound of the water was soothing. Everything has a language, whether or not humans speak it.

The park opened onto the Rosaleda Francisco Sabadell, a rose garden, one of the oldest gardens in Valladolid according to the sign, which neither Fatima nor Idris had the energy to read. The flowers looked parched, much as humans do, though not for lack of drinking. Fatima sat down on a low wall by the hedges that encircled the garden, enjoying the cool sensation of the stone through her linen trousers, and the prickle of the branches against her back. Idris sat down next to her.

On a level that neither of them yet understood, these two individuals had synchronised. Not in a physical sense, their breathing and heartbeats weren't 'as one', that's the stuff of rom coms. It's been labelled 'magical', 'spiritual', 'mystical' over the course of history. Humans, closer than ever before to truly grasping it, might now call it 'mental'. In any case, it is a rare thing to witness, this mental unity, and We savoured it.

Idris felt a nudge against his arm. He opened his eyes, which he'd closed for he had felt the urge in that moment to only listen. Before him was Fatima's hand, holding out a cigarette. He didn't refuse. After all, they were organic.

(22)

Valladolid → Nájera, Spain (215 km)

By six, they were back on the road on the final stretch of their journey to Nájera.

"Okay, Idris, new subject. I want to talk about the fourteen words we found on the scroll. I've been trying to figure out if there's a logic to their ordering on the hand. I'm convinced there must be. I've been thinking about it non-stop."

"I woke up several times last night thinking about it, too."

"So, let's start with the thumb."

"There were two words on the thumb, right? The first was *tabaq*, which you translated as 'phase', and the second was *majma* ', meaning 'meeting place'. I know these because they're from Quranic verses that I've always found fascinating, even as a kid. The first, if I remember correctly, is from a verse that describes our spiritual journey as one which will 'pass from one phase to another'. And the second is from the verse where Moses is trying to reach the point where two seas collide, a place where very strange things happen, almost like a twilight zone."

"You know, Idris, I was always jealous of people who grew up surrounded by Arabic, the things you pick up just from hearing these words in your surroundings. This is one place I'll admit your background trumps my book learning. I'd have had to look all that up."

"Oh, a rare compliment!"

"Not one you earned though! Anyway, going back. We have 'phases' and 'seas colliding'. So, why would these be on the thumb?"

"Well, I think we can assume that the thumb is the first finger, since Arabic is read from right to left. That would mean these two words might hold the clue to understanding what follows on the remaining fingers, which all have three words."

"Sort of like a key, nice. So, if these are the key… then it could mean that the words on the rest of the fingers describe phases, possibly ones that somehow collide…? Phases of what though?"

"Of our spiritual journey, of course. That's what the verse is about."

"Right, this is exciting. Let's see if it works. So, the three words on the index finger would describe the first phase, then."

"Do you remember the words?"

"Are you kidding? I told you, I haven't stopped going over them in my head since I unrolled that scroll. On the first finger, we had 'womb', 'magic' and 'speech'.

"Womb?"

"Womb must refer to womanhood, or fertility. Something related to the feminine. What else could it possibly mean? And... if these describe a spiritual journey, like you said, this must indicate a phase when the feminine was important. Have you heard of the Venus figurines?"

"Venus, like the Roman goddess?"

"No, not the Roman goddess. Modern historians refer to them as Venus figurines, but they actually date back to long before Rome and its gods even existed. Historians think they are religious symbols that go back to, I think, about 40,000 years ago or so. They've found hundreds of them, all faceless women with very large breasts and hips, symbols of fertility."

"The womb?"

"Right."

"So, a phase of goddesses then?"

"Not goddesses. More like... an age when the sacred was seen through the lens of the feminine. Not just

353

seen through the feminine, but even communicated by women too. You know, I read that the vast majority of cave art was actually painted by women. The hands you see on cave walls, they're predominantly female hands. There are caves like that all over Spain, in fact."

"That's incredible. I wish we could visit one."

"No time. But this idea—the divine feminine lens— would explain the other two words too, 'magic' and the 'spoken word'. This creative power, the power of the womb, was seen as magic, and magic is expressed through words, things like chants, and charms and incantations."

"If that's what this is really referring to, then this would be…"

"I know, I know! Let's see if we can keep going with this. So, the first word gives us an idea of how the divine is seen. The first word on the middle finger was 'he'. This fits perfectly! What came after the age of the divine feminine? Prophets, revelation, scripture. All of which predominantly refer to God as 'he'."

"Of course! The Hebrew scriptures, the Gospels, the Quran. God is always 'he' in those. I always wondered about that."

"Yes, this would be the era of Abrahamic faiths.

Moses, Jesus, and Muhammad. The age when masculine references to God take over. This explains the word 'book' too. All these religions were based on scriptures. And the 'pupil'... eyes? That could mean reading, studying, I suppose. The whole idea of formalised religion."

"Keep going, keep going. Don't stop!"

"Okay, on the fourth finger, we had 'I', 'bond' and 'heart'. 'Bond' and 'heart'... If those refer to a phase that comes after the Abrahamic religions, then I can only guess that this would be the age of spiritual mysticism that took over the world from about 1200 onwards."

"Rumi's era."

"Exactly! You're proving your worth again, Idris."

"No comment."

"Now 'I'... God as 'I'...?"

"I can answer that one, being a lover of Rumi myself. He talks about unity with God. Spiritual unity. Getting rid of the self, becoming one with God. So, there is only the 'I' of God left. It's similar to concepts found in other spiritual traditions too, like Buddhism and Taoism."

"Of course. We studied Rumi's poetry in our undergraduate classes, actually. He's one of ours by the way, all the best poets were Persian."

"Debatable."

"The Eastern traditions don't seem to be addressed by this scroll directly."

"I noticed that."

"It must be because it was intended for a specific audience."

"Right, us!"

"The crushed and disillusioned with the Judeo-Christian and Islamic traditions."

"That would make a great book title!"

"Hold on, Idris, we still need to figure out the fifth finger. This has to be our phase. The post-mysticism era."

"Life after Rumi."

"This had 'we', 'certainty', and 'mind'. So, the first word on each finger was a reference to God, or to how the divine was understood in each phase. From the feminine 'womb' to the masculine 'he' to the singular

'I', and finally to 'we'. But why 'we'...?"

"Well, the feminine and the masculine are obvious. The 'I' works with the focus on oneness with God in mysticism."

"So, the 'we'... must be a lens for our time. Not 'I', but 'we'... A way to describe just how complex 'God' really is. You know, I read somewhere that scientists still don't know why an atom can act like a wave, rather than a particle, except when being observed by the human eye. I mean, what the actual fuck? How does it know someone's watching?!"

Finally, We observe them as they observe Us, for the first time.

"I have never heard that word used in such a mind-blowing sentence."

"Are you referring to 'fuck' or 'atoms'? Idris, you know what just occurred to me?"

"Tell me."

"The names on the scroll must correspond with these phases. There were four columns. Four fingers, four phases, four columns. And the fourth column, which according to this logic would signify the phase of mind and reason..."

"The phase we are currently in."

"... was empty."

"Meaning the last name in the third column is the last representative of the phase of spiritual mysticism."

"You know who that was? That just happens to be Mencía López de Haro, the woman whose tomb we are on our way to visit."

(23)

Nájera, Spain

They arrived at the hotel just as the sun was sinking into the northern Spanish horizon. Fatima had booked two rooms at the Pensión San Lorenzo. When she had found time to do this, Idris was not sure. But she had, and the place seemed clean and comfortable. They dragged their bags silently to the elevator, keys in hand. All Fatima could think of was a bath. All Idris could think of was Fatima.

In his room, though exhausted, Idris was unable to sleep. While this was not uncommon, what was different this time was that rather than his repertoire of Playmates, all he could concentrate on were the stills he had collected that day. Fatima sitting on the wall, blowing streams of smoke into the still hot air, Fatima's face as she watched the food arrive at the restaurant, Fatima's passion as she talked about the scroll, seeing her see it in her mind's eye. This, he thought to himself, was infinitely more seductive than any Playboy centrefold he had ever seen, and he'd seen them all.

Entirely oblivious to any of this, Fatima ran a bath. She existed in that complicated space, which humans all occupy from time to time, in which, on one level, she was reassured by, even appreciated Idris's presence in the neighbouring room, whilst on another, he was completely absent from her thoughts.

For centuries, most humans have approached dreams in the same way they approach almost everything else they didn't fully understand, as a realm where illusions take over and rational thinking disappears. All one needs to do to confirm this is examine one of the numerous medieval treatises on dreams and their interpretations. Dream of a raven and you will die. A mouse in your house means, obviously, that your wife is having an affair. A few did indeed have the gift of interpreting dreams in a manner that reflected their acute understanding of actual patterns and events. But the vast majority, even today, fail to grasp the most basic aspect as to why dreams are manufactured by the brain. Dreams are, in truth, memories of events that didn't take place. To process deep and often subconscious emotions, the brain, the right inferior lingual gyrus, located in the visual cortex, creates a visual 'memory' of an event that captures these emotions and, in the process, allows for them to be vented out, as it were. We have, in truth, instilled a private and award-winning movie director in each and every human brain. This, human scientists are now beginning to understand.

Untold is the joy that ripples within Us at the sight of scientists consumed in their research, those in particular who have dedicated their lives to what most humans regard to be matters that have no direct or even indirect bearing upon their lives. The saints and mystics of this phase of human spiritual evolution can be found in the labs of deep-sea ecology and deep-space exploration centres. Just as women and men once spent hours in intense prayer contemplating Our glory, scientists now spend hours upon hours studying the intricate designs of the universe, the way in which We unfold in physical space. No doubt there are those who deny Us even as they observe Our movements within atoms and along flares racing way outside of the heliosphere. But they, you must understand, are denying how We have been shared with them by the guardians of a previous phase. To each phase, there is an image of Us consistent with human awareness, and for each phase there are guardians and rebels. We invariably entrust Our secrets to the rebels.

Our favourite human scientists are those who have the courage to think outside of the obvious, like those who dare to study what humans describe as parapsychology. You see, the brain, in the manner We designed it, is not merely a transmitter, but also a receiver. Humans have so far failed to consistently prove that it is possible for the brain to communicate without the aid of sensory faculties. They have failed because what they are trying to demonstrate is far too elusive than to be captured by their current testing techniques. We know brains can be communicated with because We communicate with them all the time, and We do so using physical space. Dreams, in fact, are one of Our most frequent ways to do this. The easiest way to understand this is to ponder upon sound. If you have lived long enough you are likely to have had a dream which was directly influenced by the sound of rain, or people talking in your bedroom, or even by the sound of an alarm clock. You are awakened by these sounds and you instantly realise, in quite certain terms, that your dream was 'rewritten' by the sound you awoke to. The only difference here is that We speak, or send Our own 'sound' waves, into the human brain. We are not an external phenomenon. We are the very blueprint of all phenomena.

Tonight, Fatima will dream of Us, once again, in the image of her Damascene spiritual teacher, dressed in a blue headscarf and navy raincoat. Fatima will walk into a mosque with Idris, but the woman in navy blue will ask him to wait outside. Fatima will open the scroll and show it to her. And the woman will smile and whisper, "To become the hand, you must let go of your own."

(24)

Monasterio de Santa María La Real, Nájera, Spain

The monastery of Santa María La Real is a building of rose-coloured stone, situated only a minute's walk from the hotel. It was founded in 1044—so the Spanish chronicles state—by the King of Navarre, over a cave in which he discovered a statue of the Virgin Mary, so far so potentially true. He was attracted to the cave, the legend continues, by a vulture and a partridge. Well, humans do love a good story.

Having paid the entrance fee, Fatima and Idris stepped into the echo-filled coolness of the monastery. It was the sort of place one could spend hours exploring, from the elaborate stone lattice walkways surrounding the courtyard to the extravagant gold backdrop in the church against which sermons—outdated almost as soon as they were spoken—would be given, to the intricate reliefs—all of men, of course—which sat atop the ornately carved wooden seating of the balcony, overlooking the church floor. But Fatima and Idris weren't there for sightseeing. Using the map handed to them by the be-gloved and masked ticket lady at the entrance, they headed straight for Doña Mencía.

Unlike most of the other knights and nobles of Nájera, Doña Mencía López de Haro is not buried in the crypt. Her tomb, rather, lies at the west corner of the monastery courtyard, set back into the outer walls behind two elegant stone columns. There is a small metal gate between the columns barring entrance to the tomb, clearly meant to deter tourists. But Fatima and Idris were no tourists. Swiftly, with a quick glance over each shoulder, Fatima slipped behind the metal. Idris followed her.

On a sarcophagus raised above her brothers' who lie at her side, Doña Mencía's effigy gazes up at the swooping stone arches, illuminated by a soft yellow light. She is depicted with her head on a tasselled pillow, the carved folds of her royal gowns spilling across the top of the tomb. She wears an ornate headpiece from which her hair flows across her shoulders. The cuffs and collar of her robes are studded and bejewelled. Fatima registered none of this.

"Where... is her hand?"

If you want to identify, discern, capture the type of intelligence that is capable of knowing Us, focus on the hand. Even cats have eyes, and even snakes have tongues. Brains won't help you either. Elephants have brains three times larger than humans. Yes, neurons are important, especially in the cerebral cortex. But you still have to account for why killer whales have more than double the number of cortical neurons than humans. No, the distinctive manifestation of Us is the hand. The grasping hand, the drawing hand, the writing hand. The hand that caresses, the hand that communicates, the hand that prays. And this was known, understood, from the very beginning. Human species long before the children of Eve, had this distinctive feature of hand anatomy, the styloid process, which separated them even from primates, and they celebrated their knowledge of being the sole living creatures entrusted with it. Caves from Indonesia to Argentina tell this story. The story of hands stencilled in red ochre, proclaiming: "With these hands, even God can be touched."

The hand is the connecting line, the symbol, the image that has survived all past phases of human spiritual evolution. From hands in figurines, to hands of statues—kings and queens—all with their hands held upright, and their palms facing outwards, facing Us.

The hand is the portal through which Our protective light is channelled, the mystery through which Our signature is confirmed. The glowing hand of Moses, the healing hand of Jesus, the water flowing hand of Muhammad, the hand of Miriam, the hand of Mary, and the hand of Fatima.

It would be impossible for Fatima and Idris to fully grasp what they had encountered, the spiritual movement of women rising against what had become a ruthless masculine religious culture that was adamant at erasing Us in the name of Us. The hand was the stubborn symbol of this movement. Jewish, Christian, and Muslim women from Anatolia and North Africa to Iberia and beyond wearing the hand around their necks, hanging the hand on their walls, even using the hand as door knockers—a sign of a home in which women touched by Us abide.

It would be equally impossible for Fatima and Idris to fully comprehend the violence unleashed against this movement, the men in black—Jewish, Christian, and Muslim—interrogating these women, even burning these women and desecrating their tombs and effigies. You know they were there, when the hand is not.

The nearest coffee shop to the monastery is Cuatro Cantones, situated at the far corner of the Plaza Santa María. Fatima and Idris had taken seats outside at a wrought iron table. Fatima had ordered two coffees, black, and she sat, eyes fixed on her laptop opposite Idris, who had followed suit and opened his too.

They could find no information on why the hand of Doña Mencía had been clearly, deliberately severed. As the empty Google search page reloaded, Fatima had an idea.

"I need you to look for medieval female effigies with

missing hands—preferably tombs."

Idris was only too keen to help. Within ten minutes of entering the search terms, he was the first to break the coffee-scented silence.

"Found one! Blanche of Navarre. Both her hands have clearly been destroyed. Her head as well."

"I found one too! Lady Constantia, wife of Grimbald Pauncefot, Lord of the Manor at Much Cowarne. Holy shit! Listen to this: 'Pauncefot fought in the Seventh Crusade and was captured by the Moorish leader, *Saladin*. According to the rather gruesome tale, Saladin told Pauncefot he would only release him if he received 'a joint of his wife' as ransom. The demand was relayed to the knight's wife, Constantia, back in England, who immediately sent for a surgeon to *cut off her hand*. The severed hand was sent to Saladin and Sir Grimbald was released as promised.' Oh my God, they're trying to retroactively explain why her hand was missing!"

"Oh wow! I found another one. Eleanor of Aquitaine, wife of the Duke of Normandy. She's buried next to her husband. His hands are both there. Her hands are completely severed. The tomb's been restored but here's a pre-restoration drawing of it, look!"

Over the next hour, We watched as Fatima and Idris came across one example after another of women We had known well, women whose postmortem punishment for daring to know Us was sarcophagal amputation.

"Here's another. Listen to this, this is crazy! Ralph Neville and his two wives, Margaret Stafford and Joan Beaufort, *both* with severed hands, whilst his remain intact. You couldn't ask for a clearer example of iconoclastic violence targeted specifically at women."

At that moment, Fatima's phone beeped. She unlocked the screen and opened the message.

"Shit."

"What is it?"

"Dr. Tabrizi, we have CCTV footage that shows you removing one parchment from the cylinder and placing it in your personal belongings. Upon examination of the cylinder this morning, we confirmed that one of the two parchments documented upon your arrival is now missing. We are left with the unfortunate conclusion that you still have this item in your possession. UK border authorities have been informed of this stolen object. You will be searched upon arrival. Please return the second scroll to the Sanctuary immediately to avoid any repercussions."

"What are they talking about? We left the scrolls there."

"Well, I may or may not have left only *one* scroll in the cylinder."

"Where's the other one?"

Fatima reached into her satchel and pulled out a

small plastic bag.

"But you signed their agreement. That specifically mentioned it would remain in the Sanctuary."

"It said the *cylinder* would never leave the Sanctuary. And it didn't. They're lucky I left them one parchment."

"But how could you have known that they wouldn't have caught you before we left?"

"I banked on them being more interested in us leaving than what we left behind. I was correct, at least initially. The question is what do we do now?"

"Well… all that message means is you can't go back to the UK with the scroll, right?"

"But if I take this back to the Sanctuary, they'll either destroy it, or lock it away. There's no way they're going to let the public know about this, they clearly know it's something important now. I mean, why were they so nervous when we found it to begin with? Why were they so relieved when I told them it was a talisman? I can't take it back there."

"Either way, all it means is that neither of us can do anything public with this anymore—no articles, no research papers. There's no way to prove it exists from pictures and transcriptions alone, and we can't reference a stolen item."

"You still haven't answered my question. What do we do now?"

"Well, it was found for a reason. And you kept it for a reason. So, the only one who can answer that question is you."

The screen on Fatima's laptop went blank for a few seconds before switching to a screensaver of old photographs. Childhood memories, graduation pictures, holidays, birthdays, her year abroad in Damascus. She reached into her bag again, this time pulling out her cigarettes. She lit one, took a deep draw, and blew out a long stream of smoke.

"I know what I need to do."

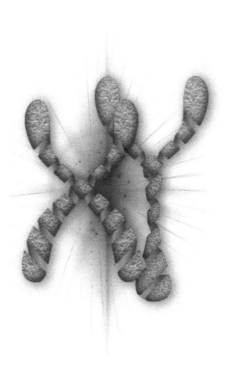

(25)

After four days of wandering around Iberia, breaking into castles, and sleeping at sanctuaries, I'm ready to return home. Home in 2020 is Southend, not Damascus, and I realise just how addicted I have become to life in my English exile. It is not difficult to make the decision to travel back by car and train. Planes, as you may recall, are my very last option. In fact, when it is possible to make a choice, planes are never the choice. And so, I hire another Fiat—why on earth are they so popular?—and I drive to Paris, and from Paris I take the last Eurostar train to St. Pancras. From there, I must take a taxi to Southend, since trains out of London stop running at midnight. Finally, and after spending a fortune, I arrive at Princess Court at two in the morning. I had informed Ana Rita that I would be arriving late, and that her gracious duties as cat-sitter would end.

I walk into my home and Lynx greets me with a look that is clearly meant to communicate her decision never to forgive me for my absence. But this won't be the first time she had made this proclamation, and it usually takes a few generous helpings of cream cheese to win her back. I had made sure to pray sunset and night prayers jointly, as I am permitted to do during travel, on the train, and so I head straight to the kitchen where I find several aluminium packages awaiting me. But I'm not in the mood for food. I just need a cup of deep dark tea to help me recover from my long trip back. I walk into my sitting room and crash on my couch. Across from me, through the window, I instantly notice, is a completely nude Ana Rita lying on her sofa with her back facing me. There's a lamp near her glowing just enough to reveal the contours of her body in the otherwise darkened room.

(26)

My eyes sink into her, and I find myself once again sat on a wall in a rose garden in Valladolid. Fatima is focused on her cigarette, and I am focused on her. It all now comes back to me. Meeting her at Mansfield College, roaming around in the dark at Castle Ourém, watching her eat, watching her speak—proud, majestic. And it occurs to me that I had not once even attempted to strip her with my eyes, to classify her within my meaningless archives of playmates and models. Not once did I pay attention to whether she was slim or heavy, tall or short, light or dark. In my mind, Fatima was so much more than this. In my mind, she was none of this. Scenes of me standing and saying goodbye returned. How awkward it all was. My silence, my desire to hold her, to make her promise she would come back. Back into my life in whatever form, in whatever capacity—just as long as she returned. I felt evicted from the comfort I had long cherished of being mentally on my own. The solitary existence that, until very recently, had been my trademark.

I open my eyes, and notice that Ana Rita has slightly moved. She is awake. Perhaps waiting for me to open the window and invite her to visit me. Little does she know that the man observing her tonight is not the man who left Southend only a few days ago. The Idris who had sat for hours anticipating her food, surveying her body—that Idris appears to have been left behind somewhere between Ourém and Navarre.

Though faint voices somewhere within me protest, I walk to the window and, for the first time since December, pull down my blinds.

(27)

Ten years ago, if you told someone you'd been to Damascus they'd think of the Bible, or scenes of sandy columns and shady souks. Now, they want to know your internet search history and whether you've made any suspicious bank transfers.

Ten years ago, I landed at Damascus airport and took a taxi into the depths of the city, mesmerised by the cacophony of car horns and calls to prayer, hypnotised by the green lights—each one a mosque—that whizzed by the window. Now, you cannot land in Damascus airport. And so, I'm on a plane to Beirut.

Ten years ago, in a restaurant in the Old City, I met a young Syrian woman with a complexion that reminded me of the rose-coloured columns of the Grand Mosque of Damascus. Seeing me struggle alone with the waiter in my then broken Arabic, she had invited me to her table and, with her melodious Syrian lilt, had ordered me a feast, for which she had insisted on paying. She introduced herself as Maryam. When she invited me to her home a few days later, I found myself sat in a semi-circle of young women on an ornate Persian rug that even my Father's family could only have dreamt of, in the midst of a fully-fledged all-female spiritual session. I had heard rumours that a spiritual women's movement existed in Damascus. I had never dreamt of finding them, let alone of them finding me. A woman dressed in a navy coat and blue headscarf was sitting on a chair positioned like a star in the crescent of women. She had started speaking. She spoke about faith with a language that, until that point, I had never encountered. It was a language of poetry, parables, even humour. I felt suspended between two melodies, the Arabic of the Shaikha, as everyone referred to her, and Maryam's English as she interpreted her words. She didn't have to ask me to come again. I was instantly addicted. For with those words the Shaikha had given me an experience of my faith that spoke to a heart I didn't even know I had.

Though my tutors' attacks on my religion were never addressed, they had ceased to matter then. I thought I had finally found an untouchable faith. It didn't take long to realise I hadn't. It was one thing to deflect the critiques of those I saw as outsiders, but it was another thing entirely to defend the loving God the Shaikha had introduced me to from my own questions. As I sat, in my final days in Damascus, and watched the choppy news stream of events from Iran unfold on my computer—the young women and men protesting the hijacking of their votes, with faces and hearts full of faith and hope, brutally silenced by men claiming to speak and act on behalf of Islam—I asked: where is God in all this? How is it possible for the God that the Shaikha had spent months describing as gentle, loyal, and tender to allow women and men of faith to be crushed in such a way? And where does that leave me? The space that faith had briefly inhabited was quickly refilled with the angry swarm of Professor Tuttle's slings and arrows, and I felt all their stings. I had left Damascus, Maryam, and the Shaikha without saying goodbye.

I had left Idris at the coffee shop outside the monastery in Navarre, having told him to go back to England. He didn't say much. Neither did I. The uncomfortable something I had occasionally felt made a brief reappearance, but was swiftly and unceremoniously dismissed. There was no time for that shit. He headed north west, and I headed south east.

I drove the car back to Madrid, left it at the car hire office, and boarded the first plane to Lebanon. A five-hour direct flight to Beirut, the nearest operating airport to Syria. When I land, I'll make the rest of the journey by road. I will let Maryam know I'm coming. I will tell her why in person. I don't have time to worry about what she'll think, or why I haven't been in touch for almost a decade.

For now, I lean my head back against the seat, ignoring the humidity of my breath behind my mask. The seat belt sign finally turns off, and I close my eyes.

God is sat to my right. She never seems to wear anything but that blue headscarf and navy raincoat. It's as though she's always prepared for rain. The stewardesses ignore her, though she's clearly violating all the laws of social distancing. She's also violating my own ten-year-old attempt to practice God distancing.

"So, you are returning. Perhaps now you will finally speak to me again."

I want to say, "I doubt it," but it seems too rude, so I end up smiling in silence instead.

I wake up to the captain's announcement that we have started our descent to Beirut.

At the airport, I send a message to Maryam. She knows I'm on my way. I hit the road immediately. Saint Paul may have entered Damascus on horseback, but I will arrive by taxi.

As a child, I had hated my father's 'tips and tricks', techniques for oiling social hinges, one might call them. My British sensitivities had always flared at the thought of bartering or bribing. And yet, here I am with an ancient manuscript stashed in my satchel. I register this irony as I slip the crisp notes into my passport and hand them to the khaki-coloured official at the Lebanese-Syrian border. I don't need any questions.

We are an hour away from Damascus. The radio is blaring the standard Syrian taxi playlist of Arabic love songs that I intermittently block out or fall into trying to translate in my head. It's as the driver leans to flick ash out of the window that the car hits something in the road, perhaps a rock or a crate that had fallen off a truck. We are thrown violently into the air, and the car comes crashing down again, swerving, then coming to a skidding halt. The driver's head must have hit the steering wheel because he's covered in blood and he is clearly unconscious. Though I'm sure there are a million sounds around me, all I can hear is the blood rushing in my ears. Concentrating hard, I can tell that the car is now in the middle of the road and facing the opposite direction, a head-on collision is bound to happen any second. It's far too dark for anyone to predict our presence in time to swerve around us. I try to move my hands, my feet. And though I know I'm not injured, I also know I cannot move. Through the car window, Syria's sky arrives, as clear as it was ten years ago, pierced by stars, and far closer than any night sky anywhere else I've ever called home. The rushing in my ears becomes a rhythm, and the rhythm becomes words:

O We of the Cosmos,
O We of the Cosmos,
O We of the Cosmos....

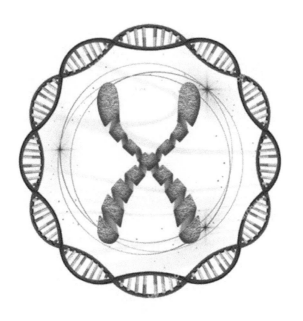

(28)

When it comes to how We intervene in human life, very few have captured what this really means. To the religious—children of past phases, stubbornly holding on to the ways in which We manifested Our presence long before humans erected flags on the moon, or scanned the brain—to them, We either reward or punish, afflict with disease or bless with a cure, bestow triumph upon the righteous or withhold victory from the unworthy. Linear perceptions which constituted a leap forward centuries ago, but that have now been simplified to the point of becoming meaningless, and often harmful. And to those who can't relate to any of this, those who are far too in tune with the intricate dynamics of this current phase of human evolution—to them, life is a function of arbitrary forces that are neither guided by an external intelligence nor purposeful in any metaphysical way. Yet another meaningless over-simplification.

To catch a glimpse of what is really at play you need to think in 3D. Observe salmon returning from the sea to the natal rivers where they were born, and even to the very spawning grounds of their birth. They proceed to swim upstream on a journey that will lead them to their deaths. Humans focus on *how* they do this, their internal compass, their sense of smell, and, interesting as this indeed is, they seldom ask *why* they would do this to begin with. To be clear, the question is not why they head upstream, the question is why they have the instinct to do so in the first place. Why the drama? Who is watching this thriller? We are. We are the storyteller, and We are the salmon and the stream. We are part of every phase of the salmon's journey, just as we are part of every phase of Fatima's. And every story We watch reveals who We are.

In humans, We have added a flow of brain energy that makes consciousness possible. And so, Fatima isn't just a salmon traveling back to its natal river because of an inbuilt instinct it has no control over, Fatima knows, as We do, what she is doing, she can see herself doing it—an external eye, as it were, that changes everything. Instead of traveling to Damascus, she could travel back to Oxford, or even back to Fátima to return the manuscript. For each choice, she encounters a different river, and a different destination. We are all these choices, and We watch the one she ultimately pursues.

And so, to understand why the car hits a rock you may begin with unsafe road regulations, move on to the careless driver. But these are merely the tangible triggers. You can't stop here, not with humans. You must move on to the realm where Fatima made the choice to return to a place which her own anger and bitterness would not allow her to experience. At this point, something takes place that is consistent with the very choice she herself has made. An accident traumatic enough to spin her out of her own trauma. You can discuss for hours whether or not the accident would have taken place regardless of whether or not Fatima was in the car in the same way as humans wonder if a tree makes a sound when it falls in a forest where no one is there to hear it. But the accident didn't happen because Fatima was in the car. Fatima was in the car because the accident happened.

(29)

Fatima was stirred in a sunny room at the Shami Hospital in Damascus by a doctor with black hair and blue eyes. In the brief moment it took for her to regain complete consciousness, she reached to his collar, pulled his face towards hers, and took his lips between her teeth, hard enough to hurt but not enough to bleed.

"*Hamdulillah 'ala salameh.* Thank God for your safety." The vision of Idris the doctor morphed into the face of Maryam, who was now standing next to the bed.

"The doctor says you are free to leave. They only kept you here as a precautionary measure. You have not one scratch on your body."

"And the driver?"

"Injured, but he will be fine. Come, she is waiting for you."

The last time Fatima had seen Shaikha Shams was in 2009 when she had still regarded herself as a Muslim believer. Today, she will walk back into the home of the Shaikha—the leader of one of the few all-female spiritual Sufi Muslim orders in history—as something very different. Not the naive young Muslim girl she once was, nor the angry and equally naive woman she later became. Today, Fatima walks into the home of Shams as the first member of a new phase of human spiritual consciousness.

Within Our scroll she had finally found an understanding of the geography of her faith, of the trajectory of Us. And this had enabled her to see Shams not as the edge of the cliff path from which she fell, but rather as a moment, a stage, a flight of the spiralling stairs that she could now continue to climb. We were why she left Damascus, and We are why she returned.

Fatima took a seat before the woman in navy blue. Maryam sat beside her.

"Do you know how the Prophet would refer to his daughter, Fatima?"

"No, Shaikha, I do not."

"He would say she is the mother of her father."

Fatima instantly noticed that, for the first time in years, invoking the Prophet didn't carry with it the flood of tense questions, and the suffocating absence of answers. She knew, in that instant, that her struggle all along had been with Us. She knew it was We who had woven the threads. We who unravelled them. The man whom she had tried for so long to defend did not need to be defended. He was already everything she wanted him to be. When We are seen, every phase is reseen.

"May you be the mother of the very path that gave birth to you."

"Your words have always touched my very soul, Shaikha, thank you. May I show you something?"

Fatima took out the scroll from her bag, unwrapped it, and placed it in Shams's hand. Looking at the parchment, Shams smiled as though she'd seen its image before.

"Shaikha, I brought this to you for you to add your name."

Shams reached for a pen from the table to her right. She removed the top and handed the pen to Fatima.

"No, my daughter, it's not me who needs to sign it. It's you."

In the fourth column, beneath the image of the hand, and the fourteen words, on parchment as old as the faith itself, Fatima signed her name.

She is the thirteenth. Only one name is yet to be signed.

"Now, go with Maryam, my daughter. She will show you where to put this."

Fatima reached to the hand of Shams and kissed it. Not too long ago, she would have recoiled from this act. But now she knew what it meant. Everything her hand is, and everything her own hand could become.

Thirty minutes later, a car parked near the Grand Mosque of Damascus. Maryam walked swiftly with Fatima by her side. They passed beneath the roman archway at the end of the souk, the remains of the Temple of Jupiter. Instead of walking into the mosque, they walked towards its southern wall. They stopped at the spot where the gate of the Cathedral of John the Baptist once stood, blocked with large stones over fifteen centuries ago. They stood beneath the inscription in Greek which still read: 'Thy dominion endureth throughout all generations.' Slowly, Fatima slid the tightly rolled scroll into the gap between two stones and pressed her hand over the opening. The scroll disappeared from sight, as though received by something on the other side.

(Epilogue)

Tell Us what you are waiting for, and We will tell you who you are.

In the year 2033, on the second Saturday of April, at precisely seven minutes to midnight, a woman in a white headscarf can be seen walking towards the southern wall of the Grand Mosque of Damascus. She can see people in the distance, congregating. She counts them. Six women, five men. Eleven. All standing at the gate of the Cathedral of John the Baptist.

She doesn't know any of them. They don't know her. Yet. But they all know why they are there. Waiting.

She had arrived in Damascus the day before. Idris, whom she had not heard from in over a decade, had written to her from Syria, where he had returned a few years earlier.

"Strange events are taking place in Damascus. Come."

She walks, as she had done thirteen years before, towards the gate, blocked with large stones over fifteen centuries ago. As she approaches, the small crowd parts, as though suddenly aware that what they were waiting for could not take place without her.

Fatima runs her hand over the stones. She finds the gap. Over a decade of dust has all but concealed it. Inserting her little finger, she feels, finds, and pulls. Slowly, carefully, she draws out the scroll.

In the way this story was once told, the wall would crumble, the gate would open.

In the way this story takes place, the extraction of the scroll causes a stone to slip. The heat, wind, rain, time—forces and elements—all play their untold parts in the tale. The wall can no longer hold. It crumbles. And so, the gate is opened.

Fatima Tabrizi is the first to enter this gate. She carries with her the scroll which bears her name as the thirteenth.

In the way this story was once told, the one to arrive, the one they are waiting for, is the Davidic King, the Messiah, the Kristos, the Son of Mary.

Christ.

In the story We wrote, We began with the feminine, the creative power of the womb, magic, water, life. We moved on to the masculine, the sceptre, the king, the crown. Next, came the inwards shift, the heart, the poem, the bond. Then, We watched the mind unmasked, the boundaries of the universe broken, reality beyond quantification, the meeting of the cortex and the cosmos. What will arrive, what Fatima will meet inside, is the synthesis, Our finale, an intelligence, a new understanding.

The fourteenth signature.

Not a woman, nor a man. But one born only to a woman. An XY from only an XX. Our final manifestation to an age beyond this age.

But that is a different story, yet to be shared.

This was the story of Fatima.

Images

All images used in this book are royalty-free images under licence or from the public domain. See full credits below.

1. (p. 87) Part of the papyri used by Joseph Smith as the source of the Book of Abraham. Public domain. Creative Commons Public Domain Mark 1.0.

2. (p. 100) A Snakes and Ladders board, author's design. Image property of Villa Magna Publishing.

3. (p. 179) Bethany Beyond The Jordan, baptism site of Jesus Christ, Jordan. Licenced royalty-free image by Ccinar, Shutterstock photo ID: 778102330.

4. (p. 303) Fatima's tracing of her own hand, supplied by Omar Imady.

5. (p. 361) Mencía López de Haro - a drawing of her effigy at the Benedictine convent of Santa María, in the Chapel of the Cross (1215-1270). Creative Commons "Mencía López de Haro" by Rufino Casado - Biblioteca Virtual de la Rioja, licenced under CC BY-SA 3.0.

6. (p. 363) Hebrew, Christian and Bohemian hamsas.

Hebrew Hamsa: licenced royalty-free image by Eddie Gerald, Alamy Stock Photo ID: P9E6HG; Christian Hamsa: licenced royalty-free image by Eddie Gerald, Alamy Stock Photo ID: P9E6G4; Bohemian Hand of Fatima, royalty-free image by Tierre3012, Shutterstock vector ID: 556280485

7. (p. 366) Eleanor of Aquitaine, Queen of England in the 12th century. Licenced royalty-free image from the f8 archive, Alamy Stock Photo ID: E525TN.

8. (p. 367) Ralph Neville, First Earl of Westmorland and his wives. Public domain. Creative Commons Public Domain Mark 1.0.

9. Chromosome drawings, owned and supplied by Villa Magna Publishing design staff.

Excerpt

Like a lab technician tasked with recording the minutiae of an experiment, I identify exactly when my last message was sent: 11:25. Next, I take note of when he was last seen active: 11:28. Three minutes. A numbness races into my fingertips. So far, it has been three minutes since he has seen my message and failed to respond. My eyelids now mutate into butterflies. Blink. Blink. Blink. Short of a massive stroke, a 7.2 earthquake with his home as its epicentre, or the arrival of extra-terrestrial amphibians at his doorstep, I can't think of a single valid excuse to justify his silence. I pace around my apartment, stumbling over objects that remind me of him. He must have noticed my tummy rolls have reappeared. As though he is in a position to judge, with his stick-out ears, and a hairline receding at a rate of approximately one inch per day. His silence, now entering its fourth minute, serves as my notification of dismissal, of my final eviction from his world.

I feel my brain matter cascade like a waterfall down my spine. I scrabble around for a Haagen-Dazs tub buried deep in my freezer. The sweat on the container forms almost as quickly as my own slick sheen as I cradle my dairy-based deliverance in my palms. I need a metaphor to help me process my pain. I'm starring in a movie that no one is interested in watching. It would be meaningless to point out that it is an award winning and brilliantly directed production. Yet, the seats in this cinema are empty, and the carpet is littered with stale popcorn. All that is left is for the lights to be put out and for the doors to be locked. Re-frozen chocolate sizzles in my increasingly parched mouth. I am slowly being numbed by an overload of sensations. 11.29. My phone rings. He's at a takeaway nearby. He figured I would be interested in pizza and another round of tabletop kitchen sex. He's asking which toppings I would like. I mumble something about black olives and onions, as I realize how incensed I now am. How dare he interrupt the intricate sequence of my fear.

CPSIA information can be obtained
at www.ICGtesting.com
Printed in the USA
BVHW071810061121
620967BV00001B/2